Y0-AZE-731

*It was late afternoon when they ... drove up
to the Catamount Tavern.*

*To my husband,
Raymond G. Fuller,
who suggested that I write this story
of his native state*

First published in 1937

Cover design by Tina DeKam

Cover art by Embla Granqvist

Illustrations by Forrest W. Orr

This unabridged version has updated grammar and spelling.

© 2019 Jenny Phillips

www.thegoodandthebeautiful.com

Contents

I. "Strange Countries for to See"...................1
II. A Night in the Woods....................11
III. Susan Makes a Friend....................15
IV. The Cabin in the Woods...................20
V. A Trapper's Tales....................28
VI. Playmates in the Wilderness...................33
VII. Blueberries and Blackbirds...................38
VIII. "Yorkers Scare Easy"....................44
IX. Much to Be Thankful For....................52
X. Hard Sledding....................56
XI. Spring at Last....................66
XII. Susan and Faith Are Left Alone...................73
XIII. Bad Pennies....................78
XIV. A Desperate Ride....................84
XV. "Nothing to Be Afeerd Of"....................96
XVI. Colonel West Soils His Shirt Ruffles...................102
XVII. A Peaceful Summer....................109
XVIII. The New Cabin....................114
XIX. The Corn Husking....................121
XX. Spring of '75....................126
XXI. A Secret That Couldn't Be Kept...................135
XXII. Susan Does Some Eavesdropping...................140
XXIII. The Call at Dawn....................154
XXIV. A Long Night....................159
XXV. The Story Jonathan Told....................164

Chapter I

"Strange Countries for to See"

Susan Eldredge stood in the jolting two-wheel cart with her back to the red-and-white oxen. Her eyes were fixed on the farmhouse at the bend of the road and on the boy and the girl standing in the yard waving goodbye to her. The two figures retreated farther and farther into the distance. Now they were only two spots of color, yet the girl in the cart still looked backward and waved her hand.

"Sit down, Susan, before you're bounced out," called back her father, who walked beside the oxen. He spoke none too soon. At that moment, the cart tipped up on one wheel as the other went over a boulder in the road. The thirteen-year-old girl lurched, clutched vainly at the dasher of a wooden churn for support, and sat down so hard on the feather bed she could feel the knobby articles it covered. There was a varied collection of household belongings under that bed—two great iron kettles, a mortar and pestle for pounding grain into meal, ears of seed corn, a cradle, and a small tin trunk. At one corner, a wooden spinning wheel projected.

"Mother," she asked sadly as a bend in the road shut out the last glimpse of the farmhouse, "do you suppose I shall ever see Rachel and Jonathan again?" To her disgust, a tear that she had tried to blink back fell *plop* on her woolen cape.

Mrs. Eldredge sat in an unpainted, rush-bottomed chair—the one chair the cart would hold—with a baby on her lap. She smiled reassuringly out of the depths of her bonnet. "Of course you will. We'll be coming back to Winfield for visits sometimes, and Daniel Lathrop may sell his farm next year and join us in the Hampshire Grants."

The road the Eldredge family was traveling that March morning in their homemade oxcart is now a smooth, wide motor road. The region into which they were moving the few belongings they could carry is today peaceful farming country in Vermont. But this was the spring of 1773, and the road was deep rutted, rocky, and perilous. Their new home was in a wilderness of deep forests, and there was no such place as Vermont.

Susan looked relieved at her mother's comforting words. "Did you hear that, Traveler?" she asked, bending over a silky black-and-tan ball that lay at her feet on an old rag rug. "Maybe you and Rachel and Jonathan and I will all play together again." A bright brown eye was visible for an instant in the ball; then it closed tightly. A small, satisfied grunt came from the puppy's throat.

Again the girl's great dark eyes were troubled. "Mother, do wolves eat puppies?"

"I don't know, child. I never heard of such a thing. Anyway, they won't get a chance to eat your puppy. We'll keep him safe in our cabin, and he shall sleep under your bed."

Now the five-year-old girl who sat on the feather bed beside Susan began to look sad as she dressed and undressed a battered wooden doll. "It's going to be a hard trip for Betsy," she said.

"Why, Faith!" protested her older sister, pretending to be

surprised. "I think Betsy is happy about going north. See how she is smiling. There aren't many dolls that have a chance to go to the Grants."

Faith looked at the fixed smile that turned up the corners of the doll's mouth as though she had never seen it before. "She does look happy," she agreed, and her own lips curved into a pleased expression. Just then, a captive rooster crowed loudly from his basket. The two girls burst out laughing and forgot to think of any more worries.

Settling herself into a more comfortable hollow in the bed, Susan looked dreamily out over the swaying horns of the oxen to the gap in the hills ahead. Somewhere, two hundred miles or more away, up above that gap would be her new home—a log cabin in the woods. For neighbors, they would have only bears and wolves and foxes. There would be no school. Everything was going to be different. And all the time the farm in Winfield, Connecticut, was being left farther and farther behind.

When she shut her eyes, she could see home as plainly as though she were still there—the frame house with its long, sloping back roof and huge chimney in the center; the apple trees her father had planted behind it; and, in front, the garden of roses her mother had tended so carefully. Again she sat on her stool by the great fire in the kitchen and smelled the fragrance of the pumpkin pies and Indian puddings her mother took out of the chimney oven on a long-handled shovel. Again she trudged to the schoolhouse where she had learned to read and cipher. Right now, even Mr. Rogers, the schoolmaster, frowning at her because she whispered would seem a pleasant and familiar sight. And the church on the village green, where in summer she had fidgeted and in winter she had shivered through Parson Bent's endless sermons, had become a place of happy memory.

Sometimes she wished Mr. Baker had never told them about the good land to be had cheap in the Grants. After that, her father had always been talking about "making a pitch" up on Otter Creek. That meant taking up land, clearing it, and building a cabin. "We'll be rich someday," he had said, "if we buy land up there now while it is cheap."

Rich! As for Susan, she was sure she would much rather be poor all her life and stay in Connecticut. Her mother would too, she knew. Why, there had even been tears in her mother's eyes that day last fall when her father had decided to take Nathan and go to the wilderness to make ready a new home. Tears in those cheerful blue eyes were a sight Susan had never seen before and never wanted to see again.

"When will I ever wear my red morocco shoes?" she asked herself and bit her lower lip to keep it from quivering. Her mother had packed them in the little tin trunk along with her own best paisley shawl and the two precious silver spoons. Yet she knew and Susan knew that they would have no use for finery or silver teaspoons in their new home.

"Whoa!" shouted Mr. Eldredge to the oxen. "Everybody out! There's a bad mud hole ahead." Seventeen-year-old Nathan left the cows he was driving and began helping his father cut down saplings to lay across what looked like a bottomless pit in the road. Susan took charge of the three cows and half-grown calf, while Mrs. Eldredge and Faith walked on ahead, glad to stretch cramped legs.

The mud hole passed, the journey went on as before till they came to a ford in the river. Then there was much shouting to the oxen and the cows and a great splashing of hoofs. The baby woke and began to cry. "Suppose," thought Susan, "it should be deeper than it looks, and we should all drown." The streams were swollen by heavy spring rains, she knew. Grimly, she held on to the edge of the cart, wondering how icy the waters would feel if they were dumped into the river. But they reached the opposite bank with the cart right-side up and everybody dry.

Sometimes their way was through woods so deep it was twilight at mid-morning. Again there was a stretch of open fields and comfortable farmhouses. At nearly every house, someone hailed them to ask where they were going. Susan enjoyed these stops. She was a heroine in the eyes of the children who had never been farther away from home than the nearest village.

"Aren't you afraid?" one girl asked her.

"What of?" Susan's voice was as scornful as though it had never occurred to her to be frightened.

"Oh, of Indians and wolves and bears."

"Father'll take care of wolves and bears and Indians with his rifle," she said confidently. "Anyway, the Indians don't trouble folks up in the Grants nowadays. They've most all gone to Canada, and those that are left are friendly. That's what Joe Barnes told Father, and he's been trapping up there for years."

In spite of the slow progress they made, the morning went quickly for the travelers. Presently, Mr. Eldredge halted the oxen by a spring, looked up at the sun, and asked, "Dinnertime, ain't it, Mercy?"

He pulled out from under the feather bed a small tin box that held a piece of steel, a bit of flint, and some dirty flax. Like a magician performing a conjuring trick, he struck sparks from the flint. Then, slowly blowing great puffs of breath, he coaxed the sparks into a flame with the pitch-soaked flax and kindled the pile of dry sticks Nathan had laid. Soon one of the great iron kettles, filled with pork and beans left over from Saturday's baking, was heating over a lively blaze. The warmed-over beans with "rye 'n' Injun" bread and milk in pewter mugs was dinner.

When they were on their way again, Mrs. Eldredge tucked Baby Joseph into his wooden cradle and began to sing to him:

> *"Lord Lovell he stood at his own castle gate,*
> *A-combing his milk-white steed,*
> *When up came Lady Nancy Bell*
> *To wish her lover good speed, speed, speed*
> *To wish her lover good speed.*
>
> *"'O, where are you going, Lord Lovell?'" she said.*
> *'O, where are you going?' said she.*
> *'I'm going away, Miss Nancy Bell,*
> *Strange countries for to see, see, see,*
> *Strange countries for to see.'"*

Susan joined in the chorus and thought of the strange mountain country she was going "for to see."

On they jolted, while the sun traveled down the sky. As it drew close to the hilltops, Mr. Eldredge began to look worried. "'Twill be nip and tuck to git to Abner's 'fore dark," he said. "Hope we won't have to camp out tonight." Now Susan began to watch the sky, for she was eager to stay the night at her uncle's house in Canaan. The sun seemed to be running a race with them, hurrying faster and faster the nearer it got to the horizon. She watched it dip below the trees—first a quarter gone, then half gone, and suddenly it was shining no more.

Frogs raised shrill voices from a pond. A cold wind blew off the hills. Susan drew her cape of walnut-brown homespun closer around her and pulled its red-lined hood down over the dark curls on her forehead. She saw how the outlines of the trees were growing blurry. Was the darkness going to beat them?

"There's the big tree," she shouted delightedly as they rounded the bend in the road. She and her cousins had often played under that old oak and in its widespread branches. It was only a little way now to the house.

"Oh! Oh!" Susan, who had been standing up looking ahead, grabbed the side of the cart just in time to keep from being hurled out as the wheel struck a stump unseen by Mr. Eldredge in the gathering dusk. In a few moments, a long-roofed, unpainted farmhouse loomed up ahead. Down the road to meet them came the old hound, barking. Traveler sat up and growled ferociously to cover up how afraid he really was. Suddenly, a path of light shone out into the dark, and welcoming voices called from the open door.

It was good to come to a stopping place after a day on the road—a day that had begun at sunrise. It was good to sit down at the long table with aunt and uncle and cousins and to spoon golden blobs of cornmeal mush into a bowl of warm milk. But the best part of the visit came when the dishes were washed and put away. Then they all gathered in a half circle before a blazing fire of five-foot logs, a fire that sent a red glow far out into the long kitchen. The women brought out their knitting, the men smoked their pipes and talked, while the young people took turns holding shovelfuls of popcorn over the coals till they had filled an enormous wooden bowl to the brim.

Susan ate popcorn and toasted herself before the blaze, feeling almost as contented as if she were at home again. A delicious drowsiness stole over her. She cuddled down sleepily in her chair and wished she could spend the night by the warm fire instead of in a chilly upstairs chamber. It began to be hard to keep her eyelids open. The voices of the men sounded farther and farther away. All at once her eyes were wide open, and she was listening hard to what her Uncle Abner was saying.

"Hope you've got plenty o' gunpowder and lead. Like as not, them land-grabbing Yorkers'll try to git your pitch away from you. Dan Parker, he made a pitch up to Shaftsbury, built him a cabin, and cleared a corn patch. He come home for the winter, and when he went back again with Mary and the children, two fellers was a-waiting for him with loaded guns, and they told him to git off their land."

"I ain't afraid o' them sneaking sons o' Beelzebub," said Mr. Eldredge, "and I've got plenty o' powder and lead to give 'em if they ask for it." He spat into the fire as violently as though he were aiming at a Yorker. "If they git too sassy, I'll send for Ethan Allen. I hear tell they're all scairt to death of him."

Abner Robinson chuckled. "I guess Ethan ain't afraid o' nothing. Never was—even when he was a boy living over to Cornwall with his folks. He was strong as a young moose then, and how he could swear! When he got started, he could cuss the bark right off a hickory tree. I don't know if it's the truth, but they tell how he would grab bushel bags of salt with his teeth and throw 'em over his head as fast as two men could fetch 'em! And I've heard how up in the Grants he once picked up a couple o' Yorkers, one in each hand, held 'em at arm's length, and knocked 'em against each other till they yelled for mercy."

Mr. Eldredge laughed. "Mebbe it's true, but it sounds a little mite exaggerated to me."

His brother-in-law nodded. "Ethan always could tell tall tales. But 'tanyrate, the governor of New York will give twenty pounds to anybody that will ketch him and bring him dead or alive to Albany. A pretty bit o' money, eh?"

"With that much money to buy land with, a man could be rich in a few years."

"And yet, with that big price on his head, nobody seems to be itching to try to lay hands on him. Why, Ethan, he bet that he could ride right over to Albany and drink a bowl o' punch at Landlord Benedict's without gitting caught. And, by Jehoshaphat, he did it. There was a crowd gathered at the tavern

Susan of the Green Mountains

to see the fun, but nobody laid a finger on him. And he rode off yelling, 'Hurrah for the Green Mountain Boys!'"

At this exciting moment, Mrs. Eldredge stuck her knitting needles into the ball of yarn and announced, to Susan's sorrow, that it was high time she and Faith were in bed asleep.

"Mother, who are the Yorkers, and will they shoot us?" demanded Susan as her mother tucked the covers around the two girls in the little back chamber under the eaves.

"No, dear, they won't shoot us. I guess Abner and your father were just swapping yarns." She spoke soothingly.

But Susan was still worried. "Who are they?" she persisted.

Mrs. Eldredge saw how wide and troubled were the girl's eyes and how flushed were her cheeks. So she sat down on the bed beside her and explained that the land called the Hampshire Grants was claimed by the governor of New Hampshire and also by the governor of New York, that both governors had granted land to settlers, and thus the same land was sometimes claimed by two different people. The king had been appealed to and had ordered the New York governor to stop granting lands that had already been settled until the dispute could be straightened out. "I don't believe, though," she added, "that Governor Tryon paid much attention to that. They've had a lot of trouble up there with the Yorkers in the past, but now Colonel Allen and his Green Mountain Boys are seeing to it that we settlers git our rights.

"Don't you worry. Most likely the only critters that will trouble us are woodchucks and foxes and—" She started to say "wolves and bears," then checked herself lest the girl should lie awake worrying about wild animals instead of Yorkers. "And weasels and all the rest of the varmints," she finished the sentence. "Most likely they'll try to eat up our corn and chickens."

Calmed by her mother's words and her goodnight kiss, Susan nestled down under the covers beside Faith. The old ballad sang itself in her ears:

> *"I'm going away, Miss Nancy Bell,*
> *Strange countries for to see, see, see,*
> *Strange countries for to see."*

In her dreams, she was pursued through deep woods by a giant of a man with a gun, who demanded that she give him Traveler. She had no gun, but there seemed to be great sacks of salt lying about. She lifted them one after another with a terrific effort and threw them at the man till he ran away.

Chapter II

A Night in the Woods

The first rays of sunlight that climbed over the treetops next morning found the Eldredge family tightly packed into the oxcart again and on their way. Susan, looking back at her uncle's comfortable farmhouse, felt like a seagoing traveler about to leave the last glimpse of land behind. She thought of the pleasant visits she had had with her cousins in the past and wondered disconsolately if there would ever be another.

This second day of the journey was one of those days that seem to have been specially selected by trouble. Joseph, the baby, wailed loudly when they started out and was fretful all day. He, too, seemed to sense that all dear and familiar things were now being left behind. After the noonday dinner, when kettles and dishes and family had been repacked and Mr. Eldredge was just in the act of cracking his whip over the oxen's heads, Susan jumped out of the cart crying wildly, "Where's Traveler? Where's Traveler?"

After a long hunt, the black-and-tan puppy was found far in the woods yipping frantically at a treed squirrel. He had to be removed from his post by force, for the idea persisted in his small, foolish head that if he waited long enough, the squirrel would obligingly come down.

"An hour lost hunting for that plaguy pup!" grumbled Mr. Eldredge as they started on their way. "If he gits lost again, he'll be left behind. We've got to make Sheffield tonight." At the mere thought of abandoning Traveler, his mistress shuddered and held him so tightly clutched that he could hardly breathe. Jonathan Lathrop had put the little fellow into her arms when he and Rachel had said goodbye to her. He was to be her companion up north where she could not have the Lathrops for neighbors.

Midafternoon brought a tragedy. It came about because Susan, tired of sitting still, offered to drive the cows. Her father turned over the oxen to Nathan and was glad to sit in the cart for a while and rest. All would have probably gone well if Susan had not seen arbutus buds poking their noses out from beneath the dead leaves and stopped to pick them. Suddenly she heard her father shouting, "Stop her! Stop her!" and saw him starting on a run after Marigold, the yellow heifer calf. She was heading for a small patch of new grass, bright green against the dead brown of the rest of the meadow. As Mr. Eldredge well knew, its greenness concealed a treacherous bog. Nathan stopped the oxen and joined the chase, but both were too late to head off Marigold. Into the black depths she plunged up to her knees. The harder she struggled, the deeper she sank.

Susan never forgot the terror-stricken look in the calf's brown eyes as she floundered in the spongy ground. "Steady there, bossy, steady. We'll get you out," called Mr. Eldredge. He and Nathan began cutting down saplings and laying them across the swampy ground so that they could reach the helpless animal without sinking in its depths themselves. But Marigold kept on floundering till all at once she sank down on her side and lay still, bellowing pathetically.

"Get the rifle, Nathan; she's broken her leg," Susan heard her father say. She turned away her head and put her hands over her ears. It was piteous to hear the calf calling for help.

She did not want to see Marigold die or hear the shot that killed her. The yellow calf had been Susan's pet almost ever since she had first stood on wobbly legs and been licked by old Brindle. But there was no such thing as shutting out the sound of the shot that went echoing through the woods. The girl hid in the bushes so that no one might see the tears that rained down her cheeks or hear the sobs she could not stop. Not till she had washed all traces of tears from her face in a spring did she come back to the cart.

There followed a long wait while Mr. Eldredge and Nathan took off the hide, dressed the carcass, and cut it up. Fresh meat was too valuable to be left behind, no matter how much precious daylight it cost. When at last they started on again, it seemed to Susan as though a member of the family were gone.

"We can't get to Sheffield tonight," Mr. Eldredge decided. "It'll be nightfall in half an hour. We'd better look for a good camping place."

Susan went to bed that night under a bark lean-to on a mattress of pine boughs. The great fire her father built made a circle of warmth and safety in the cold, black world that lay all around. Yet the girl was too worried to sleep. There were fearsome sounds in the woods. In the distance, something shrieked like a woman in agony. Susan knew without asking that it was a catamount. The howling of wolves seemed to come nearer and nearer. "There must be a whole pack out there," she thought, then took comfort in remembering how her father had once said that a single wolf would sometimes make so much noise it sounded like a pack.

She heard her father talking to Nathan in a half whisper. Raising herself quietly on her elbow, she listened tensely. "They smell the fresh meat. Have to keep a blaze up all night. Take turns watching." He was talking about wolves, she knew. Were they in great danger? Now her imagination began to work overtime. Every rustle, every branch creaking, was the sound of an animal's tread or whining cry. The owl's hoo-hooing was the howl of some prowling beast. She shivered. She pulled the blanket over her ears. She tossed from side to side and was sure that there would be no sleep for her that night. Yet nobody should know that she was scared. She would lie quiet and pretend to be asleep.

High above the sparks that rose from the fire, one star brighter than all the rest seemed like a friendly signal lantern hung up in the sky. Why, it looked like the same star Susan had seen when she had peered up the great chimney at home. It was a comforting thought. All at once, she was back there in the chimney corner of the big kitchen, sitting on the stool by the fire. Rachel and Jonathan were there too, and they were all roasting apples over the red coals.

Susan sniffed. There was a fragrance in her nostrils of wood smoke, pine needles, and boiling cornmeal mingled. The bright star was gone. The chimney corner was gone. The woods were all around her again, but the tree trunks were rose-colored on one side where the first light of day was touching them. Traveler nudged his mistress' cheek with his cold nose as if he would say, "Get up, lazy bones. Let's go tree a squirrel."

The wild animals were still. Birds sang in the treetops. They were all alive and safe. "It was silly of me to be afraid last night," thought Susan as she ate her hot mush. In her joy that the night was over, she never noticed how worn and heavy-eyed her father and mother looked that morning.

Chapter III

Susan Makes a Friend

"Why, it looks just the same as Massachusetts!" exclaimed Susan.

Her father threw back his head and laughed. "Did you think everything would look different the minute we left Massachusetts?"

She nodded. They were in Pownal, the first settlement in the New Hampshire Grants, climbing over the hills to Bennington. A week had gone jolting by since the girl had waved goodbye to her neighbors in Winfield. With a mixture of feelings, she had watched the hills grow higher and the houses grow fewer. Home seemed a great way off now, to be reached only after toiling up steep, rocky heights and pitching and lurching down again to climb up another mountain.

Yet Susan did not want to turn back. Those pine-covered hills ahead, so green and lovely in the sunshine, so black and forbidding after dark, kept saying, "Come and see what is on the other side of us." Often, when she had gone to bed at night, she would hear weird sounds from those hills—cries of the prowling creatures who like darkness better than daylight. Then Traveler would prick up his ears and growl and cuddle closer to his mistress, and Susan would shiver, as she had shivered that night they camped in the woods, and would wish she were at home again in Connecticut. Always in the morning sunshine, she would forget the fears of the night and would be eager to be on the road north again.

It was late afternoon when they came to the village of Bennington and drove up to the stuffed catamount set on top of a pole—the signpost of the Catamount Tavern. The two-story frame house with great chimneys at each end looked like a comfortable resting place. From the chimneys poured a volume of smoke that told of blazing logs in the common rooms and roasting venison and bear steaks turning on spits before the kitchen fire.

Landlord Fay met them at the door with a cordial greeting and showed Mrs. Eldredge his beds, while Mr. Eldredge and Nathan drove the cattle to the barn. Susan lingered outside the door to stand wide-eyed beneath the tawny creature that seemed to be all ready to spring down upon her. The stuffed animal had for the girl the horrible fascination a snake can exert over a bird. She tried to look away from the grinning, catlike head, only to raise her eyes again to the top of the pole. Was he daring travelers like them to come into the wilderness and be torn to pieces by those strong teeth?

"Don't you like our pet kitten, little maid?"

She started at the sound of the heavy voice and looked up to see a crag of a man leaning over from what seemed a great height. Coarse-featured, brown skinned, with power in his every movement and a swaggering step, he stood out from the men who had followed him from the tavern door, like the one peak that always seems to top all the other peaks of a mountain range.

Susan decided that she would be afraid of this man if his smile were not so kind. "No, sir," she said, looking up at the catamount again. "I think he's a horrible creature. Why do they have him on that post?"

"To scare off the Yorkers, my dear. You've no idea how wise that crittur is. He can tell one o' those land thieves 'fore he's halfway up Bennington Hill. But he wouldn't touch a hair o' your head." He laughed at his own jest—a great, ringing laugh. But Susan did not even smile.

"Will the Yorkers steal my father's land up on Otter Creek and take the nice cabin he's built away from us?" she asked gravely.

"Not if I or any o' my men ketch them a-doing of it, by—" He quickly checked the oath that rose to his lips.

"Who are you?" she asked bluntly.

"Ethan Allen, Commander of the Green Mountain Boys, at your service." He made a sweeping bow and flourished his wide, three-cornered hat.

Susan's mouth dropped wide open. Her eyes grew bigger and bigger as they traveled from one brass button to another on his coat front to the gilt epaulets on his shoulders and finally to his twinkling eyes. "Ethan Allen?" she repeated, as though she did not half believe him, then saw that he was laughing at her incredulity. "Oh, sir! Can you pick up sacks of salt with your teeth and throw them over your head? And is it true that you grabbed two Yorkers and held them at arm's length and knocked them together till they was pretty nigh killed? That's what my Uncle Abner says you did."

Now the eyes under the shaggy brows were dancing with fun. "You mustn't believe everything you hear about me, little maid. And you must remember that I'm considerable like that crittur on the pole. I do all my snarling and clawing at the Yorkers, and I can really purr very nicely. And now that you know who I am, mebbe you'll enlighten me as to what your name is and where you came from in that cart."

"My name is Susan Eldredge, sir, and we used to live in Winfield, Connecticut. But Father's sold our farm, and we're going to live up on Otter Creek the rest of our lives, I guess."

The colonel noticed the homesick look that came into the girl's face as she spoke of Winfield, and the smile he bent upon her was still kinder. "You don't say you come from Winfield, Connecticut! Why, I was born in Litchfield, 'bout a day's trip from there, if you go shank's mare. And I don't live far from Winfield now—just over to Salisbury. That is, I live down there in the wintertime, when the Yorkers go into their dens like the bears. Now, Susan, tell me where on Otter Creek your father's pitched his claim."

"Northborough's the place. Do the Yorkers get up there, sir?"

"Child, those varmints are anywhere and everywhere. But jest like all varmints, they're cowards. Remember that. And if they come bothering round your place, you jest send for me, and I'll give 'em a taste o' the beech seal they're not likely to forgit. Do you know what the beech seal is, Susan?"

She shook her head. The kind look had all gone out of his face. There was a hard, steely glint in his eyes. The girl was almost afraid of him.

"It's a flogging with a stout beech stick."

"Oh-h-h! W-where will I find you?"

The smile flashed back again. "Well, I'm anywhere and everywhere, like the Yorkers. Sometimes I'm here at Landlord Fay's. Then again, I'm at Cousin Baker's up to Arlington, or—I tell you, Susan, Shoreham's not so far from Northborough. You send a message to Paul Moore's, and I'll get it. Paul's a trapper. Anybody'll tell you where he lives. When I'm up that way, I mostly stay with Paul."

"Susan! Susan!" The disapproval in Mrs. Eldredge's voice was all too evident as she called from the tavern door.

"Good day to you, sir," Susan said quickly. Her manner was suddenly very prim.

"Goodbye and good luck to ye all." He made a deep bow, strode over to the horse block, jumped on his horse, and went galloping up the road, spattering mud in all directions. The men who had been waiting impatiently in the yard mounted and galloped after him.

"Susan, do you not know that it is unseemly for a maid to loiter about a public place talking with strange men?" asked her mother sternly.

"But, Mother, that man was Ethan Allen, and he—"

"I don't care if it was Governor Wentworth himself," interrupted Mrs. Eldredge. "It is not meet for you to be so bold. Come inside at once."

Susan had been brought up never to question her parents' opinions or commands. And yet, as she sat before the fire in the common room that evening, she was glad that she had been bold enough to linger outside and talk with that tall, homely man.

Chapter IV

The Cabin in the Woods

Susan was desperate. She wouldn't have been half so upset if the patient, mild-eyed oxen had suddenly reared up on their hind legs and pawed the air as she was to see tears streaming down her mother's cheeks. It made everything seem wrong. The woods were gloomy in spite of the bright sunlight that slanted between the tree trunks. The trail had no end.

"I'd rather it had been anything else—anything. Mother used that wheel all her life, and I learned to spin on it when I was five years old." Mrs. Eldredge stood looking down over a high ledge of rock at the spinning wheel that lay below, broken beyond repair.

"I'll make you a new one, jest as soon as we git there, a good one, too," promised Mr. Eldredge, patting her shoulder comfortingly. She tried to wink back her tears and smile, but the attempt failed. The trouble was that Mrs. Eldredge was too worn out from the long trip to stop crying once she had begun.

Ten days had gone by since they left Bennington—the hardest stage of the whole journey. There was no road now—only a blazed trail, along which the travelers plodded on foot in single file. Mr. Eldredge had made a drag out of a crotched tree to take the place of the abandoned cart. On this the family possessions had gone bouncing and slithering through the woods, and the wonder was that anything remained.

Susan thought how her mother had cheered and comforted the rest of them all along the way until now. When the baby had been so sick, she had tended him almost constantly, brewing oak bark tea for him and rocking him soothingly in her arms for hours. When Nathan wrenched his ankle, she had bathed it and bandaged it and taken her turn steadying the drag while he rode on the back of one of the oxen. She had comforted broken-hearted Faith for the loss of Betsy, when early in the trip the doll had fallen out of the cart and been smashed to splinters under the ox's big foot. These last weary days, when they had made snail-like progress and their new home seemed farther away from the old one than they ever realized before, she had kept the supply of family courage from giving out altogether by making little jokes and singing old, familiar songs.

Now that her mother was too tired to be the comforter, it was her turn, Susan decided. Joseph had begun to wail, and Faith was showing signs of sniveling. What could she say or do? All at once, the girl's clear treble went ringing through the woods:

"Two lofty ships that from ol' England sailed,
One was the Prince o' Luther, one was the Prince o' Lee
Cruisin' round on the coast of Barbaree."

As she began the second verse, "'*Go aloft*,' cried our Cap'n, '*Go aloft*,' shouted he," Nathan, Faith, and her father joined their voices with hers. By the time the ships were again "cruisin' round on the coast o' Barbaree," Mrs. Eldredge was singing, and Joseph was doing his best to qualify as a member of the chorus. So they went on, singing to keep up their courage.

"Hark!" cried Mr. Eldredge suddenly and stood still, listening. There was a sound like wind blowing through the forest. Yet there was no wind. "It's Sutherland Falls just ahead. We'll be riding down Otter Creek in a few minutes if my raft is still there."

Presently, they were looking down on a wide, foam-flecked expanse of brown water. Mr. Eldredge plunged into a thicket of sumac and emerged triumphantly dragging behind him the raft he had built the summer before. "We'll make Pittsford tonight, and tomorrow we'll be home."

Again Mrs. Eldredge sat in her armchair, and Joseph slept in her arms. The two girls were settled comfortably on the feather bed. Nathan was poling the raft along easily with the current. On the shore, Mr. Eldredge walked, driving the cattle and singing cheerfully. The long trek over mountains and through pathless woods was over. The river would carry them now to within a half mile of their cabin door.

Susan lay back on the soft bed and watched the white cotton-batting clouds that seemed to be floating lazily backward over her head. It was fun to travel like this. Never before had she known such a pleasant way of getting from one place to another. The weary days of rough going through the woods were forgotten. She looked off toward the Green Mountains that had retreated farther and farther to the east as the valley widened. They were a hazy blue now, lovelier than ever. Perhaps life up here would not be so bad after all.

Suddenly, she sat up and looked at the shore ahead of them. Something was moving among the tree trunks. No, she must have imagined it. There was nothing to be seen but the motionless trees. Yet, one of those trees wasn't a tree. It was a man, standing as though rooted there. When they drew nearer, she saw that he wore buckskin trousers and jacket and that his skin was dark. An Indian! He stood with one moccasin-clad foot poised in the air, looking now like a bronze statue, and seemed to be fascinated by the sight of the raft and the collection of articles piled upon it.

"Look, Mother, there's an Indian watching us," said Susan. She made the mistake of pointing at him with her finger. Even in the instant it took Mrs. Eldredge to turn her head, he was gone. Susan did not see him move. The earth seemed to swallow him up. One moment he was there; the next moment he had vanished.

"Look *out*!" The alarm rang across the water in sharp tones that did not sound like Mr. Eldredge's voice. Too late. Already the raft had struck a great rock concealed by the brown water and had nearly capsized. It hung there tipped at a perilous angle. The churn went rolling off and started on a voyage of its own. Mrs. Eldredge's chair pitched over. Susan grabbed it and held on while her mother, with Joseph in her arms, got a tight hold on the wet feather bed. At that instant, a piercing scream sounded. They turned to see a white, horror-stricken Faith lose her hold on the slippery logs and tumble into the river.

"Reach her the pole, Nate!" shouted Mr. Eldredge, taking off his shoes and coat and diving into the water to swim to them. Nathan managed somehow to slide it under his sister's body as she rose to the surface and at the same time to steady the raft. She grabbed the pole and clung to it like a drenched, terrified kitten while her brother pulled her out of the water.

Susan, who was holding desperately to the upper edge of the roughly built craft, clutched the shivering Faith with her free arm, expecting that the raft would founder at any moment. Would her father get there in time to save them if they went into the creek? Meanwhile, Nathan was pushing gently against the rock with his pole, trying desperately to float his cargo again without wrecking it. Scrape! Scrape! Splash! They were off the rock. Could they make shore before the water that already soaked their feet submerged them completely? What a long expanse those last few yards of river seemed!

Now Father was holding one edge of the raft and pulling them in to shore. They were not going to drown. They were safe! But Mother was trembling, and Father looked like a ghost. There was no time to think or talk of how they felt and of what a narrow escape they had had. Mrs. Eldredge undressed the dripping Faith and began rubbing her soft skin till it was pink, while Susan, whose teeth chattered like castanets, tried to quiet Joseph's loud protests against the experience, and Mr. Eldredge and Nathan hurried to gather wood for a fire.

What next? Faith had almost lost her life, and they had all had a narrow escape from ending the trip at the bottom of Otter Creek. Marigold was dead. They had lost Mother's spinning wheel and the churn. The hens and the handsome red rooster had been given to a settler near Bennington in order to reduce the load. Oh! Why had they ever come away from Winfield anyway? Thus gloomily ran Susan's thoughts as the Eldredges huddled around the fire and watched the steam rise from their damp clothes and from the waterlogged feather bed.

Nobody could sing. Nobody could even talk now. Did the rest feel as blue and discouraged as she did? Susan wondered. Then, looking from one face to another, she answered her own question with a "yes." Their spirits as well as their bodies were thoroughly dampened.

Soon Mr. Eldredge was glancing uneasily at the sun and announcing, "We'll have to do the rest of our drying off on the way, if we're going to make Pittsford tonight. Nathan can pole the raft, and the rest of you can walk till you're dry and warm."

As they began reloading their damp possessions, Susan wished with all her heart that they need never go on with this dangerous journey, and, looking into her mother's face, she seemed to read the same thought. "Only a little way now," said Mr. Eldredge encouragingly. "Almost there, almost there," he repeated every few minutes, as he saw how pale and utterly spent his wife looked and how the two girls were limping. Only his cheering words kept Susan from crying out as her damp shoes and stockings raised great blisters on both her heels.

Worn out and bedraggled, they arrived at dusk in Pittsford to rest before starting at dawn on the last lap of the long journey.

***

There was a pile of stones under a lightning-torn tree on the river bank. "Here we are!" called Mr. Eldredge. Nathan poled the raft to the edge of the water and held it steady while the rest of the family jumped ashore. Following the blazes on the trees, they made their way slowly up the wooded hillside. This was the last half mile of their two-hundred-mile journey.

Each one carried something from the load on the raft, and the oxen's broad backs were piled high. Mr. Eldredge's head was almost eclipsed by the seat of the rocking chair, which he bore on his back while carrying a small tin trunk in his hand. Nathan was pulled over sideways by the weight of the great iron kettle filled with seed corn and wheat. Susan swung a milk bucket in each hand. Faith struggled to keep her footing on the rough woods trail with a frying pan and a small kettle for her load. And Mrs. Eldredge somehow managed to hold Joseph on one arm and carry his cradle with her free hand.

In a few minutes, Mr. Eldredge stopped and pointed ahead to where the tree trunks ended abruptly in a clearing dotted by fire-blackened stumps. A small log cabin stood waiting for them to come and live in it. At their approach, a deer lifted her head and bounded into the woods, waving a white tail, and an eagle rose from a tall pine, screaming a protest over their intrusion.

So this was their new home! This was the place they had traveled all these miles to reach—a lonely, bare cabin with a stump lot for a dooryard. A lump rose in Susan's throat as she thought of the comfortable farmhouse in Connecticut with the tall elm trees bending over it and her mother's flower garden in the yard.

Yet, when her father had thrown the heavy door open on its hinges of deerskin, unfastened the bark shutter from the oiled-paper-covered opening that served as a window, and kindled a fire on the hearth, the lump was gone. Now the old rush-bottomed chair was standing on one side of the fire, while, on the other side, Joseph lay in his cradle jabbering cheerfully his own special language, and the teakettle hung on the crane, singing through its black nose the same song it had sung in Connecticut.

"It has a floor!" exclaimed Mrs. Eldredge, delightedly looking down at the rough, split logs under her feet. Most of the settlers' cabins had only the ground for a floor. The things that pleased Susan most were the table Mr. Eldredge had made by nailing half of a wide log onto a stump of a tree and her own folding bed. The table looked as if it had grown up out of the floor—a huge, square-topped wooden mushroom. The bed was a roughly built frame of wood with a bark bottom, made to fold up nearly against the wall in the daytime. For Faith, there was a trundle bed that rolled out from under her mother and father's big bed, while Nathan had to climb a ladder to the loft overhead to find his sleeping place. Mr. Eldredge's tired face lighted with a smile as he saw how pleased the family was with the furniture he and his son had worked so hard to make.

Susan and Traveler went poking and nosing about, investigating every inch of the new home—the plaster of mud and sticks between the logs, the chimney that began at the bottom as a stone chimney and was topped with a framework of small logs stuck together with mud, the cellar dug outside and covered with logs, and the bark shack that housed the cattle until her father could build a log barn.

Presently, Mrs. Eldredge began to stir cornmeal into a

kettle of bubbling water while Susan set out the pewter bowls and wooden spoons on the mushroom table. When the bucket of warm, foamy milk, which Mr. Eldredge brought in from the barn, had been strained and portioned out in the bowls, they sat down for the first meal in their new home. The yellow hasty pudding had been their daily fare for the past three weeks, but none had tasted so good since they left Winfield as did this supper, eaten at the journey's end.

The meal was over; Susan and her mother washed the bowls and ranged them on the shelf, then made up the beds and covered them with gay homespun coverlets. The girl looked around at the firelight playing on the pewter, at the baby in the cradle, at the warm colors of the bed covers, at Traveler curled up on the rag rug in front of the fire, and gave a sigh of content.

Now Mr. Eldredge threw a pine knot on the fire, took up the family Bible, drew his stool close to the hearth so that he could see the print by the bright light of the knot, and began to read from the book of Exodus of the wanderings of the children of Israel in the wilderness. Susan listened sleepily, wondering if the Israelites could have had as many troubles on their journey as the Eldredge family had had or if they were even half as glad to get to the Promised Land as she had been to reach her cabin home in the New Hampshire Grants.

Chapter V

A Trapper's Tales

At dusk one afternoon, there came out of the woods a weather-beaten-looking man whose tread was as noiseless as an Indian's. His bright, dark eyes peered from under bushy black brows, and an unkempt, dark beard covered nearly all his face. "Does he look," Susan asked herself, "more like a squirrel or a bear?"

It was their nearest neighbor, Joe Barnes, a trapper who lived by himself about three miles down the creek. Stretching out his long, buckskin-clad legs before the fire, he leaned back contentedly and poured down his throat in a few enormous gulps the tall pewter tankard of cider Mr. Eldredge brought. Then he wiped the drops from his whiskers with a dirty sleeve and began to talk. For the rest of the evening, no one else had a chance to do more than utter an occasional exclamation or ask a question. Joe was making up for all the days when he cooked and ate his meals alone and went tramping through the woods with no one but a solemn-faced old hound to talk to.

"Ouch!" he exclaimed as he wriggled in his chair. "My right shoulder allus gits the cramps a damp day like this. Yet it was two years ago that the old she-catamount clawed it up."

A long "Oh-h-h-h" came from Susan. She drew her stool closer to where Joe sat.

"'Bout this time o' day it was—little mite earlier—," the trapper went on, not unconscious of the impression he was making. "I'd been along the creek looking after my beaver and muskrat traps and was making a beeline for home, when I see three half-grown catamounts rolling over and playing together. Wal, I figured the old lady was off hunting for their suppers, and I crept up to them, thinking I'd make a pet o' the purtiest one."

"Are little catamounts really pretty?" asked the girl on the stool, forgetting in her excitement that youngsters were supposed to keep quiet while their elders were talking.

"Purty and cute as them yeller kittens o' yourn, only bigger of course. All at once, I heard a scritch-scratching of claws in the tree over my head, and I jumped three feet. 'Twas that old mother cat!" Joe looked out of the corners of his eyes and noted with sly satisfaction that Susan and Faith sat listening pop-eyed and open-mouthed. Then he went on with his story. "I'd heard her jest in time, but I didn't jump quite fur enough. One of her great yeller claws struck my shoulder as she sprung. My arm went numb, but I somehow got my old musket aimed—I don't know how. If it had missed fire, I wouldn't be here talking with you tonight. But I put a bullet right between them glittering eyes jest as she was poised ready to come at me agin.

"Then I reached for my knife, thinking that pelt o' hers would make a nice, warm bed cover, but I couldn't seem to move my arm. I looked down at myself, and by the great horn spoon my shoulder was all tore up into ribbons. My shoe was half tore off my foot, and there was enough blood on the ground to fill that kittle."

Again a gasp came from the direction of the stool. "H-how did you git home?" Susan did not see the winks her father and mother exchanged.

"How did I git home? The Almighty only knows. I crawled there somehow on my hands and knees and dripped blood all the way.

"Now don't you little gals git worried," he added after a moment, noticing signs of teeth-chattering from Faith and Susan. "The wild critturs are mostly more afraid o' you than you are o' them. There's jest two things to remember—don't git nigh a mother with young ones, and keep clear o' them in a hard winter when they're starved crazy.

"Amos Mead's wife had a close call last winter. They live down in Castleton. She was riding home from visiting her brother 'long toward dusk one afternoon, and a wolf come out o' the woods and begun to follow her. He kept a-gaining and a-gaining on her, and she got scareder and scareder. Finally she decided he meant business and was a-going to spring. She grabbed hold of a limb of a tree that hung low and swung herself up into it. The horse went galloping along lickety-cut.

"When Amos see the mare come home without Maria, he started right back, sure as Jedgement Day he was going to find her dead. But there she was perching in that tree like a turkey hen gone to roost for the night.

"Seen any Yorkers yet?" he asked cheerfully as they sat down to supper.

Mr. Eldredge shook his head. "Not a sign of one. Have you?"

"Oh, they don't bother me none," Joe replied as soon as his mouth, tight-crammed with bread and fried fish, could be used for conversation. "You see, 'taint worth their while to throw me out. I ain't got no land to speak of, and it ain't cleared—'cept my beaver medder—and my cabin's about big enough fur a chicken to roost in. What them fellers do is to wait till a settler has a nice piece o' land all cleared and a snug cabin and barn built on it. Then one o' them suddenly comes round and proves it's his, 'cause the Governor of New York says so, and he sells it agin to the settler or to somebody else fur enough so's he can go back to town and live without working fur a spell. The Yorkers—at least most of 'em—ain't honest settlers who want to come here and raise crops and families. They're land sharks. They're speculators."

"Thieves is what I call them," said Mr. Eldredge bitterly, "and so's Governor Tryon, and a rebel against His Majesty too. He's had his orders right from the king to quit granting land over here till the rights of this quarrel can be straightened out, and he keeps right on."

"That's the truth," agreed Joe, "but the Yorkers are a-gitting plenty scared o' the Green Mountain Boys. Why, Paul Moore was telling me how a few weeks ago a couple o' them brought a sheriff from Albany up to Dan'l Warner's place in Bridport and said they was going to stay there till he and his family moved out, and if they wa'n't gone in twenty-four hours, the sheriff was going to arrest them. Well, it come dusk and a hoot owl started hollering in the woods. Would you believe it—them three jumped onto their horses and started lickety-cut for home. They thought that owl was the Green Mountain Boys creeping up on them. That's one o' their signals you know—three owl hoots."

The trapper's lean shoulders shook with mirth. The Eldredges, young and old, laughed till the backless benches around the table rocked under them. Never before had the small cabin held so much laughter.

"I've seen a lot of cowards first and last. But that's the first time I ever heard of a grown man running for an owl," said Mr. Eldredge. "Them Yorkers scare easy."

"Spent all their lives in towns," explained Joe, as if that might account for anything.

Supper over, the guest filled his pipe, stretched his legs out on the hearth again, and fell silent. He had told all his best stories. In a few minutes, he knocked out his pipe and rose to go.

"You must stay the night with us," said Mrs. Eldredge. "It is late to go home. You might miss the trail in the dark."

Joe's eyes twinkled merrily. "Thank you kindly, ma'am, but

when this old fox can't find the way to his hole in the dark, it'll be time fur him to curl up his toes." He kindled a splinter of pine in the fire, lighted his lantern, and set forth into the woods, silent-footed on his moccasins.

From the doorway the Eldredge family watched his light go glimmering along the trail and heard him singing gaily:

> *"Oh, the fox and the hare,*
> *And the badger and the bear,*
> *And the birds in the greenwood tree,*
> *And the pretty little rabbits,*
> *So engaging in their habits,*
> *Have all got a mate but me."*

Chapter VI

Playmates in the Wilderness

To Susan's surprise, she was not lonely nor homesick. From the time the sunlight struggled through the trees to the cabin in the morning till it was swallowed up again by the woods at night, there was no time for a thirteen-year-old girl, especially when she was the oldest girl in the family, to think whether she was lonely or not. She scoured the pewter dishes, carded flax, and spun it into thread on the new spinning wheel her father had made. When it was time to cook dinner, she sat before the fire turning the spit so that the meat could cook on both sides or stood over a kettle stirring beans to keep them from burning. Sometimes it seemed as though her own fiery cheeks must be as well done as the dinner before it was ready.

Each day brought special duties—brewing and setting a kettle of dye for the carded flax or wool, washing the clothes and hanging them on the bushes to dry, making soap, and pounding corn into coarse meal. There was work out-of-doors for a girl, too. Susan helped her father plant corn, just as she had in Connecticut. It was fun to go up and down the newly plowed furrows, digging her bare toes into the soft earth, and dropping four kernels of corn into each little hill while she chanted softly:

> *"One for the blackbird,*
> *One for the crow,*
> *One for the cutworm,*
> *One for to grow."*

Though there were no other children to play with, there were plenty of animal companions. Traveler had changed from a silky ball into a bundle of energy attached to long, awkward legs and big feet that had grown faster than his body. He was always ready for a game of rolling and tumbling or stick chasing. In June, a new calf was born. Susan promptly named her "Marigold the Second" and taught her to drink milk out of a pail at the proper time.

One day, Mr. Eldredge came home from a trip to Neshobe riding a horse. She was dark brown, the brown of a pine tree trunk, and down her face was a long streak of white, like a newly cut blaze. So they named her "Blaze." Susan lost her heart to the mare as soon as she looked into her brown eyes and stroked her nose, a nose even softer than Joseph's velvety cheek. She rode her round and round the clearing and to the spring. Unfortunately, there was not much chance for a real ride. It was not safe for a girl to go alone into the woods, so easy was it to lose one's way.

Faith's favorite playmate was the spotted fawn Mr. Eldredge found one day in May, deserted in the woods, and brought home in his arms. He made a soft bed for him in the shed, and the little girl became his foster mother. Until he could drink without help, she fed the lost fawn by letting him suck her finger dipped in milk. In less than a month, the little fellow was nibbling grass. Early one morning, before Faith was even out of bed, the ungrateful young deer went bounding away into the forest. The little girl never saw him again, but for weeks she watched for her pet to come back.

Faith's love for animals gave Susan a fright she never forgot. Late one afternoon, the girls were playing hide and seek. It was Faith's turn to hide, and Susan had been running about for several minutes, peering behind the big boulder, the trees, the tall stumps, the house, and the shed. She looked indoors. Faith was not in the cabin. She was not in the shed. "Fa-ith, Fa-ith, come out! I'm not playing anymore," called Susan over and over. No answer! No Faith! Susan went down the trail to the spring. No Faith! There was only one place left to look—in the woods, the woods they were forbidden to explore alone.

Susan panted along the dark trail to the creek, peering among the trees on both sides. The farther she went, the more fear laid hold of her. Was her sister lost in these dim woods that stretched in every direction for miles? At the thought, such a panic as she had felt only in nightmares was upon her. Her legs were weak. All at once, the girl's heart seemed to stop beating. There, several yards from the trail in a thicket of blackberry bushes, was a small blue figure topped by a yellow head. Not three yards away from the yellow head rose above the tangle a hairy black head, as big, it seemed to Susan, as the great iron soap kettle at home.

Tearing her dress and the skin of her arms and legs, she plunged after her sister, snatched her up, though the weight of the stocky little girl bent her almost double, set the child down in the path, and started on a run, pulling her by the arm. "I want to play with the big dog," wailed Faith. "Ouch! You're hurting my arm. Let me go-o-o!" Susan paid no attention to Faith's protests. She did not even stop to explain the danger they had been in till the safety of the clearing and a resting place on the great boulder had been reached.

Then, in angry tones, she commanded, "Sit down and listen to me." The little girl looked up into her sister's staring eyes and her face that was whiter than the linen cloth that lay bleaching on the bushes and obeyed her.

"I've saved you from a horrible death, Faith Eldredge. That 'dog' you wanted to play with was a bear, and he'd have clawed

... rose above the tangle a hairy black head.

your eyes out or crushed your bones to bits if I hadn't come after you." Susan was not quite sure what a bear would do to a little girl, but she drew freely on her imagination.

Faith began to whimper at the thought of such a fate, but she stopped when Susan went on solemnly, "Now you know as well as I do that Father has forbidden us ever to go into the woods alone, and if I tell him what's happened, you'll get a whipping. But I'll never, never tell if you promise me not to do such a thing again."

"I pr-promise," sobbed Faith, who was now so thoroughly frightened she would have promised to stay in the house the rest of her life.

The truth came out at bedtime. "Why, where in the world have you been, child?" asked Mrs. Eldredge as she saw the deep, red scratches on the little girl's legs. Then she picked up the blue linen dress and inspected the three-cornered tear above the hem, which Susan had hurriedly basted together.

Faith's blue eyes were anxious. "I—I—got into some briers," she stammered. Susan, undressing in her dim corner, kept a discreet silence. By this time, their mother had discovered the long rent the whole length of Faith's sleeve, also basted together. "Why, your dress is all torn to pieces," she exclaimed. Under Mrs. Eldredge's penetrating gaze, the little girl told the whole story, interspersing it with sobs.

In silence, her mother bathed the cruelly scratched legs and arms, rubbed them with bear's grease, and mended the torn clothes. Then she inspected Susan's scratches and torn dress and prescribed the same treatment. "You were very plucky," she told her, "but if Faith ever gets lost again, you'd better let your father or Nathan go after her."

"I wouldn't punish Faith this time, Matthew," she advised her husband later. "I'm certain she won't go into the woods by herself again." And she didn't.

Chapter VII

Blueberries and Blackbirds

"Want to go blueberrying with Nate and me, Susan?" asked Mr. Eldredge one afternoon in July. "I've discovered a lot of bushes in the swamp up-creek a piece."

For reply, Susan jumped up from the spinning wheel, dropping the spindle she was filling with linen thread, and got her sunbonnet. "Can you spare her, Mercy?" her father asked, turning to Mrs. Eldredge. Susan paused in the midst of tying her bonnet strings. Her dark eyes were more eloquent than any spoken appeal could have been.

"Yes, she's been working hard all morning. I guess she's earned a change."

"Can't I go too, Mother?" pleaded Faith. "I've got my square of patchwork done." She held up the work for inspection.

Her mother looked approvingly at the neat stitches then appealed to Mr. Eldredge. "Is it too far for her to go?"

There was doubt in his face. "'Taint so far, but it's a bad bog, and you have to watch where you step. You'd better stay with your mother, Faith."

Susan was relieved at his decision. Her sister would just be a nuisance tagging along. For once, she'd like to do something without having her to look after. Then she saw the tragic disappointment in the little girl's face. She looked just the way Susan knew she would be looking if Mother had said "no" to her instead of "yes." "I'll take care of her," she volunteered, after an inward struggle with her own desire to go without her.

"Well, if you can pick berries and keep watch of Faith too, I guess it will be alright."

The two girls skipped along the trail behind their father and Nathan, happy to be free from household tasks and to be going somewhere. The long summer days that began at four and five o'clock in the morning and ended at dark were so full of milking and cooking and dishwashing and churning and spinning and weaving that a berry-picking expedition seemed like a wonderful junket. Just to walk through the dim, mysterious woods and along the sparkling waters of the creek was a great adventure to the lonely girls.

Arrived at the swamp, the fun of jumping from one grassy hummock to another and stripping the bushes of blue-black berries began. How large and luscious they were, and how good they tasted! Susan and Faith were as happy as the red-winged blackbirds that swung on the bushes, chuckling and singing, "Ock-a-lee-ee." In spite of all the berries they ate, their baskets filled up quickly. Again and again, they poured them brimming into the big kettles. When the best bushes near the edge of the swamp were stripped, Mr. Eldredge and Nathan went farther into the thick growth, picking their way cautiously over the springy ground.

"Don't try to follow us," Susan's father told her. "You stay right near that clump of tamaracks. We won't be long."

The girls refilled their baskets, then sat down on a hummock of moss and picked them over. A blackbird perched over their heads and scolded them severely. "We must be near his nest. Let's leave our baskets under the tamarack trees and see if we can find it," suggested Susan. They poked about among the bushes and reeds, lured by the canny bird from one clump to another, farther and farther away from the place where the nest was hidden. That spot remained a secret between Mr. Blackbird and his brown mate.

"Why, where are those trees?" exclaimed Susan when they gave up the hunt and came back to what she thought was their starting place.

"Over there," said Faith, pointing to some tamaracks several rods away.

"I didn't think it was in that direction," said Susan. "I must be all turned around."

When, after jumping over many a black bog, they came to the tamaracks, there were not baskets of berries under them. "What could have become of them?" the girls asked each other. Then, looking up into the tree beneath which she stood, Susan made a painful discovery. "These are the wrong trees," she decided. "The clump we hid the berries under were taller and had one dead tree in the middle."

They turned around and started back in the direction they had come from. After a long series of jumps from hummock to hummock, Susan looked up to see the trees they had, as they thought, left behind them. So they were going around in circles. That was what people always did when they were lost. A sick feeling came over her as she looked around. In every direction stretched blueberry bushes, all looking exactly alike. Was there any end to this miserable swamp? From which direction had they come? Which way had Father and Nathan gone? In vain, she looked for the other clump of tamaracks and for the rock Faith had perched on when she was tired. They were lost—lost in the swamp. All the color went out of Susan's cheeks. She had visions of wandering about like this till dark and spending the night perched on one of the hummocks in this bog.

Well, she mustn't give up, and she mustn't let Faith know how scared she was. Again they started out. This time, she knew she was heading in a different direction from the way they had gone before. They pushed through bushes and jumped over bogs for half an hour. Still nothing looked familiar. At least they had not gone around in a circle. But they were lost—lost in a sea of bushes that went on and on like the waters of a real sea. What was the use of wandering around anymore? Better stay right here and hope that Father would find them before dark. But what if he didn't?

All at once, she remembered something her father had told them. On their first trip to the Grants, he and Nathan had lost their way in the woods. "I looked for the tallest tree in sight," he had said, "climbed it, and looked around till I got my bearings."

Was there any tall tree that she could get to? Or was this just a world of bushes, bushes, bushes? All the tamaracks seemed to have disappeared now. She peered over the bushes in every direction. Yes, away over there she could see what looked like the top of an oak. Could she get Faith there and back? At any rate, they must keep together. "Where are we going?" asked the little girl as Susan took her firmly by the hand and started for the tree.

"Over there," said her sister vaguely, not wanting to discourage her at the start.

"Is that where our berries are?"

"Perhaps."

Soon Faith was complaining that she was tired and didn't want to go any farther, for she had no idea how desperate was their situation or why Susan was so determined to walk. Susan kept on in a straight line, sometimes carrying Faith over bad places, sometimes stopping for a moment to let her rest. Once she slipped and went up to her knees in the black mud. It was all she could do to pull her legs out of the heavy, sucking mire. "I mustn't do that again," she told herself, "or I'll meet the same fate as poor Marigold did."

The tree appeared to move farther and farther away. Faith kept begging to stop and rest. Would they ever get there? It seemed hours to the tired, worried girl before they came up on the higher ground where the tree stood. Thank goodness it was still there. Susan had half expected to find that it had moved again.

"You stay right on this rock, Faith," she told her sister. "I'm going to climb the tree. Perhaps I can see where Father and Nathan are."

The little girl was only too glad to sit down on the rock and was too tired to ask questions. "I'm glad I was a tomboy and learned to climb trees," thought Susan as she carefully worked her way from one branch to another. Peering through the leaves now and then to make sure that Faith had not wandered away, she came at last to an opening made by a dead branch near the top. This was her observatory.

Anxiously, she looked out over the wide landscape that opened before her stretching in every direction toward blue hills. Heavens! How they had been wandering around! Why, there were the first tamarack trees where they had left the berries, as far away again as they had just come. They had been going in just the opposite direction. How would Faith's tired legs ever hold out to get clear back there and home again? What a fool she had been to ask Father to let her sister come anyway. If it wasn't for her, getting out of this mess would be much simpler. Susan's irritation at Faith was the greater because she knew in her heart that the "mess" was her own fault. She had suggested looking for that silly blackbird's nest. Down on the ground again, she took stock of herself. Her legs ached. She was dripping with sweat. She had lost her sunbonnet. But she could make it, if only Faith could.

The return trip was like a nightmare. Susan had to steer her course carefully by the sun, keeping it over her left shoulder just as she had marked her way from the top of the tree,

Susan of the Green Mountains

or she would get turned around again. The going through the swamp seemed harder than ever now that she was tired. The hot sun beat down on her bare head, and the flies bit cruelly. Every few minutes, Susan would carry Faith "pig-a-back" for a while to rest the short legs that threatened to give out altogether. Would her own legs hold out much longer? If ever she got home again, she never wanted to see another blueberry swamp so long as she lived.

"Yoo-hoo-oo!" It was Father's voice. It had never sounded so good to her before. "Yoo-hoo-oo!" she called. Their voices rang back and forth across the sea of bushes till Mr. Eldredge and Nathan came in sight of the two girls.

"You children scared me out of twenty years' growth," said their father sternly, mopping his wet forehead with his sleeve. "I thought you were both swallored up in the bog. Where on earth have you been, and why didn't you stay where I told you to?"

Susan, feeling altogether silly, related her story—the bird's-nest chase, its unhappy consequences, and what she did when she found they were lost.

"Well, of all the tarnal foolishness! Chasing around in a swamp like this after a bird's nest. But I'll say one thing for you. You didn't lose your head, as most would have done. Yes, you showed a lot of sense at the end. But mark my words, Susan, if you ever want to go anywhere with me again, you've got to obey orders and stay where I tell you to. These woods and swamps are no places for wild-goose chases or wild-blackbird chases."

Susan agreed with feeling that they were not, and wearily she followed Nathan and her father along the homeward trail, while Faith, who by this time was completely worn out, rode on Mr. Eldredge's shoulder. She and Faith were learning things about the wilderness, Susan decided, but it was a painful business.

Chapter VIII

"Yorkers Scare Easy"

Blaze turned her white nose around and looked anxiously at her master, as if she were saying, "How much more are you going to put on my back?"

"Fetch that sack o' wheat, Nate," said Mr. Eldredge, "and we'll be off." As he spoke, he was fastening two bags of corn securely to the saddle. "We won't be back till late tomorrow, Mercy. With this load, we'll have to ride and tie, and there's no telling how many will be ahead of me at Crippen's mill. Then I've got to git a new shoe put on Blaze and take back 'Liphalet Barker's broad axe."

He mounted with the axe over his shoulder and rode into the woods. Nathan followed on foot. He was to walk the first few miles, then his father would tie Blaze to a tree and leave her for Nathan to ride the next lap. Thus they would "ride and tie" all the way to Pittsford and back.

Susan's heart was full of envy as she stood in the yard and watched her brother's retreating back. Life was unfair to a girl, she thought. Nathan had all the adventures. He went fishing and hunting and to the mill with his father, while she stayed at home and cooked and spun and sewed.

It was September. Many changes were to be seen around

the log cabin. The clearing had widened. Each week saw a few more trees topple under the busy axes. Many of the stumps had been burned out so that there was something like a dooryard in front of the cabin. The hollyhock seeds Susan had brought from Connecticut and planted by the door had sent up strong green stalks that would bear columns of pink blossoms by another summer. Shocks of dry cornstalks stood where Susan had dropped kernels of corn in the spring. The wheat patch was yellow stubble. A log barn stood ready to shelter the cattle from winter blizzards.

Inside the cabin were two new chairs and a stool made of hickory wood and hickory-bark seats that Nathan and his father had made on rainy days. The big loom was set up in one corner, and on it a woolen blanket was growing in preparation for the cold northern nights that were coming. Mrs. Eldredge and Susan both worked on it whenever they could snatch a few moments from immediate duties. Faith helped too, keeping the bobbin wound with the firm wool thread she had learned to spin.

It seemed to Susan, as she swept out the cabin that morning, that she had lived here in the woods for a long time. It was home to her in a sense that the Connecticut farm had never been home. She was seeing the desolate cabin in a stump lot change into a place that was pleasant and homelike, and she was helping every day to bring about that change. How she had hated to come! Yet now she never wanted to live anywhere else.

"I guess we've got enough fat to make some candles," said Mrs. Eldredge, "and today will be a good chance to do it." She pulled out from the chimney cupboard the kettle in which for months she had been hoarding every bit of bear's grease, deer suet, and moose fat she could skim from frying pan and stew kettle.

The two girls began tying at intervals along sticks the strips of wicking their mother had made ready for candle-making day. Meanwhile, Mrs. Eldredge kindled a fire in the yard and hung the kettle over it. When the fat was melted, she took one of the sticks, dipped the wicks quickly into the kettle, and handed them back to Susan, who placed the "dips" across the backs of two chairs to cool and produced another set for her mother to coat with grease.

Susan always had enjoyed a candle-making day. It was fun to watch the candles grow fatter and fatter with each dipping and to think how many things they could do winter evenings by the beautiful light they would give.

"Mother! Who are those men?" Faith, who had been standing by the kettle looking on, pointed to the edge of the woods.

Mrs. Eldredge's hand shook as she gave Susan another stickful of dips. She was looking at the two strangers and at the surveying instruments they carried. The candles fell out of the girl's hand to the ground and broke into pieces. But she did not even notice that she had dropped them. Her eyes, too, were on the men who had appeared so suddenly. They looked quite different from the homespun-clad men she had seen in the Grants before. As they came nearer, she noticed that they wore white shirts with ruffles and that their coats were of fine cloth trimmed with shiny silver buttons.

What was it she had heard her father say about the Yorkers? "Those dressed-up dandies never plowed a field or milked a cow in their lives, and they don't intend to soil their hands or their fancy clothes with honest work."

"Well, my good woman, where did you come from, and how long have you and your little brood been living here?" The older of the two strangers spoke in a patronizing and insolent tone. Susan had never seen her mother's face so white or her eyes so blazing. "She knows they're Yorkers, too," the girl decided.

"What is it to you where we come from and how long we

Susan of the Green Mountains

have lived here? Who are you, and what is your business?" The voice was scarcely recognizable as Mrs. Eldredge's.

"I beg your pardon, ma'am. We should have introduced ourselves." The man spoke with a mock politeness that was even more insulting than before. "I am Colonel West, and this gentleman is my brother. We are making a survey of this bit of country. You see it just happens, unfortunately for you, ma'am, I admit, that we own this land you have so coolly appropriated."

"And how long have you owned this land?"

"For a couple of months."

"Then we have the prior claim. My husband made his pitch a year and a half ago."

"Yes, by the authority of one of those Connecticut land companies that has a so-called charter from Governor Wentworth. We know all about that, and we also know that their charter for this land isn't worth the paper it's writ on. You poor people are victims of fraud."

"I see we are." Mrs. Eldredge looked straight into the speaker's narrow gray eyes till his mocking glance shifted uneasily from her face to the ground.

"And now, if you'll excuse us, we must get on with our work," he said, assuming a bustling manner. "We shall expect you and your family to be packed up and out of here by the end of next week."

"We'll see about that."

Mrs. Eldredge went on dipping candles as if there had been no interruption. But the color did not come back to her face, and her hands still trembled. She watched the two strangers from the corners of her eyes.

Susan thought of the tall commander of the Green Mountain Boys and wished that he would suddenly come out of the woods and pick up these two little dandies and knock them together till they begged to be let go. All at once she seemed to hear Joe Barnes saying, "They jumped onto their horses

"We own this land you have so coolly appropriated."

Susan of the Green Mountains

and rode lickety-cut for home. They thought that owl was the Green Mountain Boys creeping up on them."

To her mother's utter amazement, Susan left her post by the kettle, walked over to the woods, cupped her hands to her mouth, and let out a loud, "Hoo-oo-oo," then another and another. She stood looking expectantly into the woods, yet, at the same time, she missed no move the two men made. At the first hoot, both of them jumped. At the second, the younger brother dropped his compass. At the third, they started toward her. Susan was glad that her dress was long and thick. Otherwise, they might have seen that her knees were knocking together. She did not dare look at her mother and Faith.

"Is this some kind of a game you're playing, child?" asked the colonel. His tone was amused, but his eyes were anxious.

The girl hung her head and stammered as though unwilling to reveal a secret. "S-sort of a-a game." She continued gazing intently into the woods.

The two brothers looked at each other questioningly, then both peered about in all directions. Suddenly, the colonel pulled out a pistol and pointed it at Susan. "Now perhaps you'll explain what all this hoo-hooing is about," he said.

"It—was—just-a-a-signal." They must see how she was trembling, thought Susan. Now her mother was standing beside her.

"If you'll put that pistol away and stop bullying my daughter, I'll explain everything," Mrs. Eldredge was saying.

Oh! Was her mother going to spoil it all just as her trick was working so well? Didn't she understand? If only she could whisper in her ear.

Colonel West lowered the pistol but continued to hold it in his hand.

"You arrived at a good time for us, sir," Mrs. Eldredge continued. "Colonel Allen and his men camped last night a quarter of a mile from here on their way to Skenesborough.

And we happen to know that they haven't broken camp yet."

At these words Susan, for the first time in three long minutes, drew a breath. The pompous man seemed actually to be shrinking in size. The pistol went into his belt. "How many of those outlaws are around here?" he asked.

"Only six," replied Mrs. Eldredge cheerfully.

"Six! I'd sooner meet six catamounts or even six devils as six of those lawless rowdies." The brothers snatched up their instruments and started for the woods at a walk that was so rapid it was almost a run. "I warn you, ma'am," called the colonel over his shoulder, "this is our land, and we shall be back to take possession of it. We may bring a sheriff or two along next time."

"They look like two scared rabbits," said Mrs. Eldredge scornfully. Susan sat down on the ground quickly, for her legs refused to hold her up any longer. "Why, Mother, I didn't know that Colonel Allen and his men really *were* near here last night. I was jest pretending. How did you know? Did Father see them?"

"I didn't and they didn't and he didn't. May I be forgiven for telling a lie, but it had to be done. You're the quickest-witted girl in the Grants, Susan. You thought of the one way to scare a Yorker—tell him the Green Mountain Boys are coming."

That night, Susan lay awake in bed for a long time. Every snapping twig, every loud rustling of wind-stirred leaves, every unusual sound made her strain her ears to listen for the possible return of the Yorkers. Suppose they should discover that they had been fooled and should come back? Mother was tossing and turning too. Was she worried? At last, too tired to listen for Yorkers any longer, the girl fell asleep and knew nothing more till her mother called her at daybreak.

The next night when Mr. Eldredge and Nathan came home, there was maple syrup for the cornmeal mush, as a celebration of Susan's victory over the Yorkers. "You and I ought to have been here, Father," said Nathan in the superior, older-brother tone he often assumed toward his sister. "They wouldn't have had a chance to point any pistols at us, would they?"

His father smiled. "Perhaps it's jest as well we weren't here. Seems to me Susan knows exactly how to handle Yorkers."

For the next few weeks, the whole family watched the trail into the woods. Mr. Eldredge wore a pistol in his belt and kept his rifle propped up against the wall near the door. A week, two weeks, five weeks went by. November came and with it flurries of snow and sharp weather. Still the Yorkers had not made the promised return visit.

Chapter IX

Much to Be Thankful For

Five appetizing fragrances, all distinctly different, rose from the hearth of the cabin. The partridge, turning golden brown in the frying pan, gave forth an odor that made every member of the Eldredge family take deep, appreciative sniffs. From three iron kettles issued smells that could be sorted into boiled turnip, boiled pumpkin, and Indian pudding. The fifth nose-tickling, mouth-watering fragrance came from the yellow johnnycake spread on a board tipped up before the fire. Mrs. Eldredge and Susan bustled about stirring first one kettle, then another, and prodding the meat to see if it was done, while Faith laid a cloth of creamy, homespun linen over the rough table and set out pewter plates and spoons.

"Seems so Grandma and Grandpa ought to come riding into the yard any minute now," said Susan.

Her mother paused in the midst of making gravy to reflect, "It's the first Thanksgiving dinner ever I cooked that they didn't help eat. I s'pose they're with your Aunt Mary today."

As they spoke, someone was heard outside whistling cheerfully:

> *"Oh, the fox and the hare,*
> *And the badger and the bear,*
> *And the birds in the greenwood tree—"*

A knock sounded on the heavy door, and Joe Barnes, their Thanksgiving guest, seemed to blow in with a gust of frosty air. "Ah-h-h-h!" He drew in a grateful breath of warmth and fragrance, pulled off the muskrat-skin cap of his own making, and began to unwind the long woolen tippet that was wrapped round and round his neck. Having shed his great coat, he drew a chair close to the fire, so close that Mrs. Eldredge and Susan could hardly keep from stepping on his long, broad feet.

"There's a few apples I brought ye—off my own trees that I planted the year I come up here." He pointed proudly to the basket he had set down on the hearth.

There were exclamations of delight from Susan, Nathan, and Faith.

Before they sat down to dinner, Mr. Eldredge opened the great Bible to the 136th psalm and began to read, "O give thanks unto the Lord; for he is good: for his mercy endureth forever." The psalm ended, he made a long prayer, naming all the things for which the Eldredge family should give thanks—abundant food, good crops, protection from the perils of the wilderness, not forgetting to mention that "the Lord had put fear into the hearts of the Yorkers and caused them to flee." It was as lengthy a prayer, Susan decided, as Parson Bent's Thanksgiving prayers used to be. But she found it easier to listen and to feel thankful sitting here comfortably on a stool by the fire with the smell of dinner in her nostrils than it had been on a hard bench in the chilly little meetinghouse at home with only a few coals in a foot stove for warmth. And if you wriggled or whispered, the tithing man might come and tap you on the head with his stick.

Yes, there were many pleasant things about this Thanksgiving Day, she thought as she ate partridge breast and listened to Joe Barnes' best bear story. After dinner, they sat around the fire and cracked butternuts and ate apples and butternut meats till there was not a chink or a cranny inside them left unfilled.

Susan and Nathan played fox and geese and checkers on the floor with red and yellow kernels of corn. Faith dressed the new Betsy Father had made for her in a gay calico dress and pretended to give her a Thanksgiving dinner. Joseph built a fort of corncobs.

In the late afternoon, the gray skies began to spit forth an occasional soft flake of snow. This was a signal for Joe to wrap himself up again. "It's a-coming right out of the nor'east," he said. "I don't take no chances with a nor'easter. Did you ever hear tell 'bout the time that 'Liphlet Mead was found froze stiff not half a mile from his cabin over on the Lemon Fair River?" he asked as he began winding the tippet round his neck. Stopping in the middle of this operation, he settled down by the fire again.

"It was a day jest like this. The air looked like you could cut it up into gray chunks and fry it like cold hasty pudding and felt like it was trying to git at your marrer bone. It hung fire fur hours, not doing nothing but looking thicker and grayer all the time. 'Liphlet, he'd been to Pittsford to git his corn ground. When he started home from the mill, it was spitting a little 'bout the way it is now. He figgered he could beat the storm home easy, but 'fore he was halfway there it begun to drive right out o' the nor'east and to come pelting into his eyes. Prob'ly couldn't see a foot ahead o' him. I recollict how I was out that afternoon myself looking at my traps, and 'twas jest like a curtain hung down all round. And wa'n't that snow heavy! Seemed like my snowshoes weighed as much as a sack o' corn apiece. Well, 'Liphlet got clean off the trail and went wallering round and round in circles fur hours, I guess. When it begun to grow dark, his folks was terrible anxious. His brother and his oldest boy, they started out with torches and went calling through the woods. But it was his old hound dog that found him—under most a foot o' snow."

Joe seemed to regard the story as finished and got up and

began to button his coat. Susan waited in suspense. "Was he dead?" she asked finally.

The trapper nodded. "Froze stiff as them fire tongs." He pulled his cap over his ears and lifted the wooden latch. "Well, good night to ye all and pleasant dreams." His cheerful whistle mingled outside with the shriller whistle of the wind.

When Mr. Eldredge and Nathan came stamping in from milking the cows, they left a trail of snow across the cabin floor. By suppertime, the knife-edged wind had driven the family into a little huddle around the fire. They hung up quilts from the beams to shut out the draughts that swept in between the cracks. The blazing logs that Mr. Eldredge piled higher and higher were powerless to warm more than a small semicircle around the hearth.

Mrs. Eldredge filled the long-handled warming pan with coals and ran it up and down the icy bed blankets. She heated stones till they hissed, swathed them in woolen cloths, and tucked one into each bed. Nathan brought his cornhusk-filled mattress down from the loft and slept before the fire.

In the morning, the cabin door could be opened only a few inches until the huge drift of snow that blocked it had been shoveled away. Through the opening the family looked out on a world they hardly knew. Gone were the stumps and boulders. Gone was the little bark shack. The house and barn were half buried. Thus, suddenly and in deadly earnest, the northern winter descended upon the wilderness.

Chapter X

Hard Sledding

To the family in the little cabin, it seemed that first year as though winter were fighting a battle with them. He tried to bury the cabin and its occupants by piling foot after foot of snow on top of it and around it. He attempted to blow it down with great winds that roared through the treetops, shrieked outside the door, and forced themselves through every unstopped crack and cranny in the walls. At night, wolves howled on the edge of the clearing as they waited for a chance to spring upon a cow or calf or even a human that might stray from the protecting walls of barn or house.

The Eldredge family fought winter's attack with every weapon they possessed. Mr. Eldredge and Nathan shoveled away and tunneled through the great snow drifts. They went back and forth, back and forth, from the woodpile to the fireplace with logs so long and so heavy it took both of them to carry one. When they were not shoveling snow or carrying wood or looking after the stock, they were swinging their axes to replenish the ever-shrinking woodpile.

Indoors, Susan and her mother stuffed the cracks in the walls with rags, hung up blankets and quilts around the fireplace, heated stones and filled warming pans with coals, and kept knitting needles clicking to supply the family with warm stockings, tippets, and mittens. To add to their work, all the food froze solid and had to be thawed before a meal could be cooked.

It was a desperately lonely life, as well as a hard one. A great white silence was all around them, broken only by an occasional cracking of the icy crust, a "plop" of snow falling from an over-weighted tree, or the chirp of hungry chickadees. Of all the birds that had sung and nested about the cabin, only the chickadees were brave enough to stay, chattering about, picking up the crumbs and scraps Susan and Faith threw to them. Even the crows had gone farther south. It seemed to Susan as though their harsh caws would be cheerful sounds now.

For several weeks, Joe Barnes failed to put in an appearance. He was too busy going the rounds of his traps and hunting, and he was too tired from his long, cold trips to visit his neighbors. When at last he came scrunch-scrunching into the clearing on his snowshoes, he was not quite his usual cheerful self. His talk was all of the weather and his own troubles, for he had seen no other human being since the deep snow came. He had nearly frozen his thumb off. His rheumatism was bad, though he had worn a horse chestnut in his pocket ever since fall, and that had always cured it before. It was going to be an "extry" long winter. He could tell by the muskrat pelts.

Early in January, there came a sudden thaw. Susan and Faith, in their homespun capes and red knitted hoods and mittens, joined the chickadees in the yard. It was fun just to run back and forth along the tunnel that led through the drifts to the barn, to race each other to the spring and back, and to flounder in the tracks of the oxen on the trail into the woods. They rolled up a great snowball. They chased each other with moist handfuls of snow while Traveler barked gleefully and ran after each missile as though he were supposed to retrieve it.

From the woods, where Mr. Eldredge and Nathan were taking advantage of the mild weather to fell a few more giant trees, came the ringing strokes of axes. Whack! Whack! Whack! The blows were like a rhythmic accompaniment to the girls' play. All at once, Susan realized that the axes were silent, that they had been silent for several minutes. She stopped in the midst of shaping a snowball to listen. No sound came from the woods. She threw the ball at Faith. There was still no whacking of axes. Not a sound! The little girl's return shot struck Susan full in the face as she stood, forgetting to duck. The silence had been broken by a voice. It was Nathan calling. Instantly, Susan started on a run for the cabin. Traveler bounded after her, sure that a new game was about to begin. "Mother," she panted as she burst into the house, "Nathan is calling from the woods."

Without saying a word, Mrs. Eldredge threw a shawl over her head and shoulders and strapped on a pair of snowshoes. Meanwhile, Susan had her snowshoes on. "What's the matter? What's happened?" asked Faith as she saw the fear in both their faces. But they did not hear her. Swiftly they ran into the woods following the tracks of the oxen between the stumps. "We're coming, Nate, we're coming!" shouted Mrs. Eldredge in answer to his call. Anxiously, they peered ahead through the trees. All at once, to their relief, they heard the "splosh, splosh" of the oxen's heavy feet in the slushy snow and the sound of sled runners coming toward them. Perhaps everything was all right after all. But everything was not all right.

Both Susan and her mother knew it the instant the ox team came in sight. Nathan was walking beside the sled and on it lay Mr. Eldredge, motionless. As the team drew nearer, Susan saw that her father's face, usually so ruddy, was as white as the snow that lay around them and that his leather leggings were red with blood. Her heart seemed to miss a beat as she looked at the still figure. Was he breathing?

"Axe slipped—cut his leg open—tied my tippet around tight's I could—thought at first I couldn't git him onto the sled alone," Nathan explained in short, jerky sentences. His face was almost as white as the face of the man on the sled.

"You run along ahead, Susan, and stir up the fire and fill the teakettle," said Mrs. Eldredge, partly because she knew that plenty of hot water would be needed and partly to distract the frightened girl's attention from her father. Susan ran as though the injured man's life depended on her speed. It was a relief to feel that she was doing something, even if it were merely filling the teakettle.

Joseph and Faith were the only members of the family who slept much that night. Mrs. Eldredge and Nathan were up all night long, alternately loosening and tightening the tourniquet around Mr. Eldredge's leg to stop the bleeding, putting cold packs over the wound, and, every few hours, pouring down the patient's throat the hot venison broth Susan had prepared. It was her job to keep the fire blazing and the kettle filled and to see to it that the broth was always piping hot. Between these duties, she sat perched on a stool by the fire, tense and frightened. She did not need to be told that her father was in grave danger. A glance at that face the color of ashes in the candlelight told her how nearly spent was his strength. Even when she heard her mother whisper to Nathan, "It's stopped bleeding at last," the girl knew that the fight for life was not over.

Finally, too restless to sit still any longer, she threw her cape around her shoulders and went outside into the cold, white moonlight for a moment. Never had the black woods looked more beautiful and never more lonely. It made her shudder to think how helpless they were here in this wide expanse of snow, hemmed round by the deep forest. She drew her cape closer about her. There was a knifelike edge to that breeze. Trained by her father to notice signs of changes in the weather, she saw that a great ring of clouds circled the moon and that the wind had veered toward the east. Was another blizzard coming to add to their troubles?

Around midnight, at her mother's bidding, she lay down with her clothes on to rest, but her sleep was broken by fearful dreams, and long before daylight she was wide awake. It was a relief when the long night was over and it was time to cook the cornmeal mush for breakfast. They ate hungrily and in silence, their thoughts with the man who lay so quietly on the bed in the corner. "Is Father going to die?" asked Faith in a whisper as she and Susan cleared the table and washed the dishes.

"Of course not. He's better already," whispered Susan, as though such an idea had never entered anyone's head.

Yet she herself did not know whether or not their father was out of danger. Nor did she dare ask any questions of her mother, so long as she went about silent, her face so drawn and tense. But when, later in the morning, Mrs. Eldredge leaned back in her armchair and fell sound asleep for a few minutes, Susan felt sure that the worst of their worries were over. There would be no such thing as even a cat nap for Mother as long as Father was in danger.

That night the rats and the mice must have put on a grand celebration, for the cabin had never been so still before. The peace that follows release from intense anxiety settled down over the place and its occupants. Everyone, including Mr. Eldredge, slept heavily. The storm that had hung out its signal the night before came slanting out of the east before midnight, the fine flakes falling with a grim determination, silently, steadily. Breakfast next morning was a much more cheerful meal than it had been the day before. The patient sat up in bed and ate his breakfast, prophesying cheerfully that he would "be lively as a cricket in a day or two."

The growing drifts outside had a sobering effect on Nathan and Susan, for they had been out and knew how fast the snow was piling up. Already Susan's arms ached from helping clear a path to the barn. "Troubles never come singly," she had heard her mother say. They certainly hadn't this time. With all the extra burden of work indoors and out that Father's accident had put on their shoulders, why, oh why, did more snow have to fall? She comforted herself with the thought that perhaps by tomorrow Father would be up and about again.

Mr. Eldredge was not out of bed the next day. That same evening, spots like red coals kindled in his cheeks, and he began to complain that his leg hurt and his head ached, that he was too hot and then that he was cold. A deep furrow came between Mrs. Eldredge's eyebrows when she undid the bandage and looked at the injured leg. The furrow stayed there in the days that followed and left on her forehead a line that never was erased.

Again a candle burned in the cabin all night while the worried wife poulticed her husband's swollen leg and kept cool cloths on his burning forehead. Meanwhile, a raging wind blew outside, hurling the snow against the cabin as if determined this time to bury the family forever. Susan lay awake for a long time listening to the storm and wondering how she and Nathan would ever get to the barn to do the chores. She did not dare to think what would become of them if anything happened to Father.

The next day was like a long nightmare. Everyone, with the possible exception of Joseph, knew that a life-and-death battle was going on in their midst. Mrs. Eldredge was in almost constant attendance on the sick man. Faith did the dishwashing and much of the cooking. Outside, Nathan and Susan fought against the stinging, snow-laden wind to keep paths cleared to the barn and to the woodpile, fed and watered the stock, milked the cows, and brought in logs for the ever-hungry fire and kettlefuls of snow to melt down for water. Getting to the spring was out of the question. Although the snow had stopped falling sometime in the night, the wind kept on filling the air with snowflakes, obliterating the paths as fast as they were made, and packing the drifts harder and harder. There was little let-up all day to this backbreaking work. Yet, though nearly every bone in Susan's body was aching by afternoon, the girl was thankful that there was so much to do. It gave her no time to think about Father and how utterly dependent they were on their own efforts to keep him alive, here in the wilderness in the midst of a raging blizzard.

There followed another night of watching and nursing. The wind went down shortly after sundown and with it the temperature to a low point for the winter. Susan began to wonder how much of sleeplessness, of toil, of worry, and of cold the Eldredge family could stand. She looked at her mother's face, white and drawn in the candlelight, and realized that at least one member of the family was near the end of her endurance. "You must git some sleep tonight, Mother," she told her. "Nathan and I can keep the fire going and look after Father. If he's worse, or if we need you, we'll wake you right away. Please lie down, anyway."

"I can't sleep a wink," her mother protested, "but I'll lie down jest a few minutes." Before the "few minutes" were past, deep sleep had taken possession of her, and she lay for hours like a drugged person. Meanwhile, Susan and Nathan took turns stoking the fire, heating stones for Mr. Eldredge's bed, and changing the poultices on the swollen leg. First one would doze on the armchair, then the other. Thus, somehow, they got through the night. Never did the boy and girl forget those desperate struggles to wake from sleep or the numbing cold that crept in through the walls even to the fireside.

In the morning, when Mrs. Eldredge put her hand on the sick man's forehead and took the poultice from his leg, a hopeful look came into her face. "He's not so feverish, and the swelling's beginning to go down. I thank Thee, God!" she said. By afternoon, the family began to relax a little, to speak in natural tones, and even to smile occasionally. That night the mice ventured out again.

Mr. Eldredge's wound healed slowly, and the strength he had spent in fighting for life came back only after a long convalescence. It was two weeks before he could even hobble about the house, and winter was nearly over when he was able to take up his full burden of work again. While he fretted at being "a useless cripple," the family somehow managed to carry on through the coldest weeks of the whole winter. Never before had Susan realized how many buckets of water and how many loads of wood had to be carried, how many forkfuls of hay must be crammed into the mangers for cattle, in the course of one day.

She was always tired nowadays, except when she first woke up in the morning. The grave expression in her brown eyes and the dark hollows under them made her look like a little old woman instead of a fourteen-year-old girl. Even strapping Nathan showed the strain of being the only able-bodied man of the family. By the end of a day's work, his broad shoulders were stooped and his cheerful whistle was still. Faith, who did more dishwashing and cooking and churning than she had ever undertaken before in her short life, was no longer the red-cheeked, bright-eyed girl she had been a few weeks before. Mrs. Eldredge looked at her daughters anxiously and decided that they "both needed a good dosing with thoroughwort tea." The announcement was greeted with groans. How they hated that bitter brew!

The climax of Susan's discomfort that winter came on the morning she and Nathan shoveled out a path to the spring. It was one of those still, sparkling days. The snow was so cold and dry it squeaked under their feet. In spite of the heavy knitted mittens and stockings they wore, their toes and fingers ached with the cold. Susan jumped up and down and slapped her hands against her side to keep them from freezing. Ouch! Suddenly she forgot her toes and fingers as her nose began to tingle and ache. Then, presently, it felt better, and she thought no more about it until Nathan, turning to speak to her, suddenly exclaimed, "Land sakes! Susan, your nose is froze." He grabbed up a handful of snow and began rubbing the small nose that now was the color of a tallow candle.

"I'm going into the house and git warm," said Susan.

"Don't you go in by the fire yet," he ordered, holding her tightly by the arm and keeping on with his heroic treatment till the nose was fiery red, and Susan cried out as it prickled.

What a looking object that red and peeling nose was for the next few days, and how sore it was! For the rest of the winter, Susan had to treat it kindly, pulling her woolen tippet over it whenever she went out in the cold.

Presently, food supplies began to run low. The salted bear meat and venison, though used sparingly, soon gave out. So did the cornmeal. And Nathan had no time for hunting. Three times a day they ate bean porridge or boiled beans and samp, the latter made from corn pounded laboriously into pieces in a wooden mortar.

Life would not have seemed quite so bleak during those weeks had there been any neighbor to drop in with a bit of gossip or cheerful talk. Even Joe Barnes was not heard from for over a month. When finally he came whistling into the clearing on his snowshoes, the Eldredges hailed him as though he were a long-lost relative.

"Wonder you didn't bleed to death," he told Mr. Eldredge after solemnly examining the injured leg. "That's what happened to George Bennet down to Neshobe last winter when he was making a clearing." He was off on one of his tales of wilderness tragedy, a tale that made his listeners shudder because it described what had so nearly happened to them.

Joe, too, had almost died a couple of weeks before, according to his own account. "Never had such a cough in my hull life. Sez I, 'Joe, you've got to fight this tooth 'n' nail, or it's going to git you sure this time.' Like enough I wouldn't be setting here talking to you now, if I hadn't had plenty o' cider on hand. I drunk all the hot cider I could take and went to bed and jest sweat it all out. Next day, I was tending my traps."

Mr. Eldredge grinned. "Some folks jest can't kill themselves no matter how hard they try," he said.

"Well," said Joe, when at last all his winters' tales were told, "high time I was going about my business. I guess the backbone o' the winter's broke now." Putting on his great coat and pulling his fur cap well down over his ears, he departed, leaving this cheering thought behind him.

Chapter XI

Spring at Last

For the first time since Thanksgiving Day, the cabin door stood wide open. The sun stretched a long rectangle of yellow light across the rough floor as if it were trying to rival the fire on the hearth. Around the stumps in the yard were wide rings of bare, brown earth. The drifts of snow that had almost buried the cabin had shrunk to the size of anthills.

"Oh, Mother! Faith! Come quick!" called Susan as she fetched a bucket of water from the spring. "Hear the bluebird!"

They stood together by the woodpile with eyes alight, listening to the sweet warble that seemed like the voice of spring itself. Joseph toddled after them, crooning delightedly, "Birdie, birdie, birdie!" The long winter was over. Susan had another sign of spring to report. "Sap's running lickety-split. The bucket on the big maple is half full already."

"Yes, it's good sugar weather," agreed her mother, while Faith ran from tree to tree to investigate for herself.

"Splosh! Splosh! Splosh!" The sound of horse's hoofs striking the soft snow came from the woods. Mrs. Eldredge and the two girls started and looked anxiously toward the blazed pine tree that marked the trail to the creek. Joseph stopped his happy crooning. Traveler barked nervously.

Susan of the Green Mountains

"Halloo-oo! Halloo-oo!" It was a call as cheerful and friendly as the bluebird's. No Yorkers this time. Who could be coming? A horse's nose appeared between the trees before its rider was visible. It was a sorrel nose with a white star. "Why, it's Starface," they cried in one breath.

Mrs. Eldredge picked up Joseph and followed the girls, who had started on a run to meet the sorrel horse. On his back was now plainly visible a man clad in brown homespun surrounded by bulging saddlebags and sacks, and beside him on foot was another figure, slighter and shorter. A whoop of delight came from the boy on foot. He tossed his cap high in the air.

Mr. Eldredge and Nathan left their axes driven into the tall hemlock they were felling and hurried to meet the visitors. "Hello, Dan. Hello, Jonathan," they called across the stump lot. "We're almighty glad to see ye."

"Where's your pitch? Are you going to stay all summer? How's Abby? When are you going to bring her and the children up?" The questions came faster than Mr. Lathrop and Jonathan could answer them.

There was little work done that spring day. The Eldredges and the Lathrops sat in the cabin for hours talking of all that had happened in the year that had passed since they said goodbye in Winchester. Mr. Lathrop's pitch was only two miles away. He and Jonathan were going to clear a small plot, build a bark shack for the summer as quickly as possible, then go back home and return with the family.

"Seems almost like Thanksgiving Day," said Susan as they sat down to dinner. There was venison steak and johnnycake and maple sugar. But it was not the good dinner that made the day seem festal. It was the familiar faces and voices—a little bit of old Connecticut here in the cabin.

When dinner was over, Susan showed Jonathan all her favorite places and possessions—the spring, the great rock,

"Halloo-oo! Halloo-oo!"

Susan of the Green Mountains

the barn where Blaze and Marigold the Second were the chief exhibits, and the two giant pine trees and the needle-covered stone beneath them, where she liked to bring her sewing and knitting. Both pines were marked with the broad arrow, a sign that they were reserved for the king's navy. "Someday they'll be masts on great ships and go sailing across the ocean and up the river to London, Father says," Susan told him with a sigh, "but I hope it will be a long time 'fore anybody comes to cut them down. I love them so."

Traveler from time to time sniffed inquiringly at Jonathan's boots. "He doesn't know you. I guess he's forgotten he was born in your barn."

"Well, I wouldn't know him either," laughed Jonathan as he patted the long-legged, floppy-eared hound. "And his mistress has grown almost as fast as he has."

Susan smiled. "I come up to Mother's shoulder," she said proudly, "and I'm 'most fifteen; that is, I'll be fifteen in September."

Jonathan's blue eyes twinkled. "At that rate I'm 'most sixteen. November's only two months further off than September. Anyway, whether you're fourteen or 'most fifteen, you're smarter than any girl I ever heard of. The way you scared them Yorkers off! Whew-ew!" He made up for lack of words with a long whistle. "I thought girls always fainted or had hysterics when they got a scare like that."

"Not girls like me," declared Susan.

"I'll race you to the dead tree and back to the door," she proposed suddenly to cover up how self-conscious she was beginning to feel.

Jonathan's long legs brought him in ahead, but only by one leap. "If I don't look out," thought Mrs. Eldredge anxiously, "I'll have a tomboy for a daughter." The race over, the two sat on the doorstep and drank sweet maple sap from a gourd and talked on about the two most interesting subjects in the world—themselves.

That night and for several succeeding nights, Mr. Lathrop and Jonathan slept on the hay in the barn. By day four, axes battled with the deep forest up-creek as the neighbors joined forces in a clearing bee. Joe Barnes, on days when he was not tramping about with his rifle or setting his traps, lent his strong arms to the task of making a home for the Lathrops. One by one, the trees that had been growing for centuries came crashing down. Others were girdled by cutting off a ring of bark around the trunk and left to die of their own accord.

The bark shack they built for summer quarters was like a great hollow tree growing out of the ground. As a matter of fact, it was not so much larger than some of the centuries-old trees that surrounded it. "I declare, it looks real nice," Mrs. Eldredge decided, when she and Susan had put the one room in apple-pie order. They had brought over stools and benches and bed quilts on Blaze's back from their own cabin and had made everything ready for the family.

"Seems like a house for a little brown bear or a beaver or something like that, it's so little and woodsy looking." This was Susan's opinion.

"They'd better lock it up tight or like as not they'll find that old Bruin agrees with you," laughed her mother.

The next day, Jonathan and his father started on the long trek back to Connecticut. As soon as the Eldredges had waved the travelers goodbye, they began counting the days before the whole family would be there. Every morning at family prayers, Mr. Eldredge asked that the Lathrops be guarded from all perils by day and by night on their journey. And every evening Susan, before she went to sleep, added to her prayers a special request, "Please take care of Jonathan and Rachel and all the rest of the Lathrop family."

Early in May, when the trees were unfolding small russet-green leaves and the grass was sprinkled with purple violets, the Lathrops reached their new home. Again Jonathan's joyous whoop came ringing out of the forest across the clearing, and Starface's sorrel nose appeared in the opening by the blazed pine.

Jonathan had ridden ahead like a courier to be the first to bring word of the family's safe arrival. "They'll be here in two shakes of a lamb's tail," he announced, considerably exaggerating the speed of the travelers' approach. He looked hopefully at Mrs. Eldredge and added, "I thought mebbe Susan would ride back with me to meet 'em."

"Yes, child, you may go, but smooth your hair and put on a clean kerchief and pinafore first."

Susan ran into the cabin and made a lightning change. She could hardly stand still while her mother tucked a few unruly curls neatly under her bonnet and retied more carefully the pinafore strings. Then Jonathan lifted her up to a seat behind him on the pillion, where she perched sideways, holding on to the saddle with both hands. No one would have guessed, to see her sitting there so demurely, how excited Susan was. At least no one would have guessed it, unless he had peeped under her bonnet and seen that her cheeks were as pink as the swamp honeysuckle buds in the woods and that her eyes were a-sparkle.

"Be sure to tell them to come here for dinner," Mrs. Eldredge called after the riders.

Starface trotted quickly along. In a few minutes, they were on the Otter Creek trail, heading southward. The waters of the creek teemed with life this spring morning. Wild ducks conversed noisily and stood on their heads in pursuit of their lunches. Kingfishers went rattling across the stream. Red-winged blackbirds swung on the branches of the trees singing, "Ock-a-lee-ee." Muskrats and otters slid quietly into the water, leaving long ripples behind them.

At any other time, Susan would have been fascinated to watch the goings and comings of the creek population, but now her eyes were intent on the trail ahead. The mooing of a cow announced the approach of the travelers. Susan and Jonathan rounded a bend in the trail, and there were the cattle plodding along with Rachel waving a stick behind them, and the raft poled by Mr. Lathrop, floating close to the bank. What shouting back and forth and waving of hands followed!

Rachel and Susan twined their arms about each other and walked along together, while Jonathan and Starface took charge of the cows. The two girls had so much to say that it seemed only a few minutes before they were at the foot of the dead tree that marked the trail to the Eldredge cabin. Here Nathan and Mr. Eldredge stood waiting to go on up-creek to the new pitch and help unload the raft. Susan and Rachel went skipping up the dead-tree trail to help Mrs. Eldredge cook the welcoming dinner.

For once, turning the spit before the hot fire did not seem like work to Susan. There was company coming. There would be company coming often now. Already the forests that stretched in every direction seemed friendlier and less dark.

Chapter XII

Susan and Faith Are Left Alone

Mr. Eldredge slung a bulging knapsack over one shoulder and a powder horn over the other. Nathan stuck his hunting knife into his belt and shouldered another knapsack. "Don't look for us 'fore the end of the week, Mercy. We may have to go even further than Pittsford," said Mr. Eldredge. "And you can't hurry pigs and sheep, you know. There won't nothing hurt ye. If anything goes wrong, send word to Dan; he'll come and help you out. Be sure and bolt the barn door and the cabin door at night. Goodbye, Mercy. Goodbye, Susan. Goodbye, Faith. Give Father a kiss, Joseph."

Picking up stout staffs, the two started for the woods, driving ahead of them yearling steers and old Brindle. They were off on a trading expedition and were planning to bring back a few sheep and pigs. Then Mrs. Eldredge and the girls would have a new supply of wool for weaving next winter's clothing, and there would be hams and fat sides of bacon for the family larder.

Susan and her mother, as they watched the two broad backs disappear among the brown tree trunks, felt suddenly small, insignificant and alone. It was the first time they had been left alone in the woods for more than one night. Fortunately, they had little time to think. The water in the iron kettle behind the cabin waited bubbling and steaming for the family washing. By mid-morning, the bushes and grass were covered with cream-white homespun sheets and towels and snowy pinafores and blue and brown shirts and dresses. Even Faith's small hands were kept busy spreading the smaller pieces of clothing to dry, helping Susan weed the flax bed, and feeding the little chickens.

There was no break in the succession of tasks indoors and out until the sun had dropped down into the woods. By that time, Susan and her mother had milked and watered the cows, strained the milk and set it to rise, fastened the barn door, and shut tight the chicken coop against prowling creatures. When the supper of cornbread and warm milk had been eaten and the pewter bowls washed, all were ready to go to bed. Joseph was sound asleep in his high chair, and Faith was nodding on her stool. Traveler, who had been zigzagging and circling about in the woods all day on the trail of a wary old fox, lay stretched out on the floor seeming to be dead, except when he suddenly twitched a paw.

Drooping their shoulders wearily, Susan and her mother went about the last tasks of the evening—undressing Joseph and tucking him into the cradle he had nearly outgrown, burying the red coals and embers deep in the ashes to keep them alive till morning, letting down the bed in the corner, and pulling out the trundle bed. Finally, Mrs. Eldredge took down the musket that hung above the fireplace and stood it against the wall beside the door.

"Ah-h-h!" sighed Susan. How good it was to stretch out her tired legs. No springy, modern bed could have seemed more grateful to the tired girl than did her hard, corn husk–filled mattress that night. She thought she was going to sleep at once, her eyelids felt so heavy. Yet she didn't. There were so many little sounds inside and outside the house—sounds she had never noticed when her father and Nathan were at home. Those pad-padding steps—were they a bear's? No, the skunk that was raising her family under the woodpile must be out foraging. What was that in the chimney? Just some soot falling. Could it be a rat that was making all that noise? What was Traveler growling about? Or was it Blaze stomping?

Finally, she gave herself an imaginary shaking, covered up her ears and began counting sheep. Before fifty wooly backs were over the wall, Susan slept. The next thing she knew, her mother was calling, "Come, child, it's time you and I were up and milking the cows." Their day was beginning before the sun was out of bed, when even the birds were just waking up and twittering sleepily, for they had more to do than the sun or the hard-working, nesting, feathered people.

They had just finished milking and were turning the cows out to pasture when Faith came flying across the yard. "Jonathan Lathrop's here," she told them. "He said he wanted to see you, Mother, and he looks like something dreadful had happened." Leaving Susan to put up the bars of the pasture lot, Mrs. Eldredge hurried to where Jonathan stood holding Starface by the bridle rein. One glance at his white, anxious face confirmed the little girl's words. "What's wrong, Jonathan?" she asked immediately without even stopping to wish him good morning.

"It's Mother. She was took bad last night. And this morning she's all burning up and don't know any of us. It's lung fever, Father thinks. He's gone over to Crown Point to see if he can git a doctor, but it may be too late by the time he's back. Seems like she was gitting worse every minute."

"I'll come right back with you," she said, answering the boy's unspoken question, and hurried into the cabin. Taking a pair of saddlebags from a hook, she stuffed one with her nightgown and some clean aprons. Into the other went bunches of dried herbs from the fragrant store that hung from the rafters.

Susan stood in the yard, first on one foot and then on the other, and wished she could think of something comforting to say to Jonathan. "Mebbe 'tain't lung fever," she ventured presently. The boy did not hear her. She was not sure he had seen her at all. Most of the time, he seemed to be staring into the woods and yet not seeing the woods.

She tried again. "Mother'll make her well. She's a wonderful nurse. 'Member how she cured Nathan when he 'most died o' lung fever?"

"Oh, Susan, I hadn't ought to take her off and leave you and Faith alone this way," he said, suddenly conscious for the first time of the plight of the two girls. "But I don't know nothing else to do. Father and Rachel and I, we've done everything we can think of, and it don't do no good." Again his eyes looked off into space. He had forgotten she was there.

"Don't you worry a bit about us. We'll be alright." Susan forced herself to speak confidently and cheerfully. But the effort was wasted. He did not hear her. His thoughts were back upcreek in the bark shack. Susan gave up the role of comforter and went into the house to help her mother.

Two solemn-faced girls stood on the steps watching Jonathan lift their mother and Joseph up onto the pillion, mount, and ride away into the woods. This morning, Susan did not feel "almost fifteen." All at once, she felt like a timid little girl left alone in a world where almost anything might happen. At the pit of her stomach, something cold and hard lay. It was fear.

"Are—are you scairt, Susan?" There was a catch in the questioning voice. Faith was looking intently into her sister's face.

"Scairt? What's there to be scairt of? Everything's jest the same as when Mother's here—except that you and I've got more to do. Come on, let's see how fast we can skim the milk and git the churning done. If we're quick, mebbe we'll have time to play a game o' hide and seek this morning. And we'll have maple sugar to top off our victuals this noon."

It was amazing how quickly the little girl went to work. To Susan's surprise, her own little-girl feelings vanished, and the cold stone in her stomach melted away, as she pretended to her sister that she "wasn't scairt." Traveler came trotting out of the woods in high spirits, home from an early-morning hunt. At the sight of his cheerful, wagging tail, Susan threw her arms around his neck, planted a kiss on his soft forehead, and whispered in his ear, "You'll take care of us, won't you, Traveler?" He flop-flopped his tail against her legs as much as to say, "I will."

She was glad there were so many things to do. Keeping busy made her forget that miles of deep woods lay between them and anyone else. It blotted out the memory of that look of dread in Jonathan's eyes. She skimmed the thick yellow cream from the pans of milk and emptied it into the churn; then she set Faith to plunging the churn dasher up and down while she made the bed, swept the floor, and brushed the hearth clean of ashes with a wild turkey's wing.

"What's that?" Faith dropped the dasher and went outdoors to listen. "It's a horse," she called in to Susan. "Do you suppose they're coming back?"

Susan followed her. Both girls stood with their eyes fixed on the opening by the blazed tree, hoping to see Starface's sorrel nose. But the horse's nose they saw was black. And from behind him came the sound of the hoofbeats of other horses. Louder than the thud-thud-thud of the hoofs was the pounding of Susan's heart.

Chapter XIII

Bad Pennies

Susan had never seen that black horse before. Yet somehow she knew who was on his back even before she glimpsed the fine coat with shining buttons and the white shirt ruffles he wore and before she recognized that sharp nose and the narrow, close-together gray eyes. One by one, they emerged from the woods—the colonel, his silent younger brother, and a large, pompous-looking man whom Susan labeled at once "the sheriff." All three had rifles slung over their shoulders.

Traveler went to meet the little procession on the run, barking enraged protests punctuated by deep, rumbling growls. "Stop that noise, you awful hound," yelled Colonel West. Thereupon the hound barked the louder. Leaping from his horse, the colonel drove a heavily booted foot into Traveler's ribs. The sound of the poor dog's yelps of pain made Susan lose all fear for herself. She flew across the yard to where the three men were now tying their horses to the trees. "You let my dog alone. Don't you dare touch him again!" she commanded, as though she had a body of armed troops standing behind her ready to back up her orders.

A contemptuous smile curved down the corners of Colonel West's thin-lipped mouth. "Hoity-toity! What a little spitfire for such a pretty baggage! Eh, Charles?"

"A Green Mountain Girl," agreed Charles with a sneer, "who needs a spanking as much as the Green Mountain Boys do."

Now Traveler came crawling painfully back to his mistress' side, growling threats at the men.

"You tie up that hound, or we'll set him up as a target and fill his belly with bullets." Colonel West unslung his rifle as he spoke.

Susan lost no time in dragging Traveler away to the house and tying him to a bedpost. "You did the best you could to look after us," she told him, patting his head and looking sorrowfully at his swollen ribs, "but it was three men and three guns against a girl and a dog. Now jest lie there and keep very quiet for a while."

Faith stood just outside the door, white-faced and staring, looking as if her legs were rooted in that spot. "Come in and go on churning like there hadn't nothing happened," Susan whispered in her ear, "and try not to act scairt."

Meanwhile, the West brothers and the sheriff were making a little tour of the premises. Susan went to the spring for a bucket of water in order to watch their movements. Rage boiled within her as she saw them walking about inspecting the young corn, the wheat, the barn, and pacing off the size of the cleared land. Oh! Why had Father and Nathan and Mother all gone away, just when they were so needed?

In a few minutes, the three men came trooping into the house. "Where's your mother?" asked the colonel when they had sat down, taken out their pipes, and made themselves thoroughly comfortable.

"She's nursing a sick neighbor."

"Where's your father?"

"He's— he's—" She hated to let this dog-kicking brute know that she and Faith were alone. "He's away on business. But he might be back soon," she added hastily.

"Well, if he's not back before tomorrow, he'll find a nice airy cabin without any roof on it."

The pewter plate Susan was scouring with rushes dropped to the hearth, cracking from rim to center. "You—you're not going to tear the roof off right over our heads?"

Again that unpleasant smile drew down the corners of Colonel West's mouth. "That depends on whether your heads are under the roof or not. I should strongly advise you to have them out as soon as possible."

Susan walked across to where he lounged indolently in her mother's rocking chair. Defiance darkened her eyes and tensed her straight little back. "You shan't touch this cabin!" she said.

At the sound of desperation in her voice, Traveler rose from where he lay a prisoner and growled savagely. Reluctantly, he lay down again when Susan commanded him to be quiet, but he continued to grumble and mutter deep down in his throat.

The colonel laughed—the most unpleasant laugh she had ever heard, the girl decided. "If I were you, my child," he said, "I wouldn't argue with three men, all armed, not forgetting that one of them is a sheriff." He flicked an imaginary bit of dust off his shirt ruffle with thumb and finger, as though he might dispose of her in the same easy manner. "Squire Putnam here has a warrant to arrest and jail anybody who interferes with my brother and me in taking possession of our property."

"But," persisted the girl, though she well knew that talk was useless, "you've got a Yorker warrant. The laws of the New York Colony ain't the laws of the New Hampshire Grants."

At this point, the stout man was heard from. "You shall see what New York law is like," he said, jumping to his feet.

"Better sit down, Squire. Don't waste your breath on a sassy young-un." It was the colonel speaking. "The first thing we want is some breakfast." He was talking to Susan now. "And I hope your cooking is better than your temper, child. We've ridden a long way on empty stomachs. You'll find some bear steaks, a wheaten loaf, and a parcel o' tea in that saddlebag on the floor. Now you jest hold that little tongue if you can and fry us some meat and boil a pot o' tea."

Susan bit the tip of the "little tongue" to keep it from making an angry retort. So they were going to stay here and make her cook for them, were they? She'd see about that. Bear steak and wheaten bread for breakfast! What luxury! Why it was a feast. And tea! Her mother hadn't had a cup of tea since they left Connecticut, except sage and sassafras tea, and that didn't count. Anyway it was wicked to drink real tea, now that the king had put a heavy tax on it.

Rebelliously she filled the teakettle and swung it over the fire. Rebelliously she turned the thick steaks in the skillet. Faith set out pewter plates and mugs, her lips set and her eyes tearful. The three men sniffed the aroma from the skillet like dogs sniffing a fresh scent. Their mouths watered as they tasted the juicy steaks in imagination.

They did not see the sudden look of desperate resolve in Susan's face as she bent low over the fire. Her full skirt screened the quick twist of her wrist that sent the slices of meat into the hottest part of the fire. "Oh! Oh!" she cried out, pretending to be almost beside herself with distress and mortification. "See what I've done. See what I've done, jest as I was taking them up for you, sirs." The smell of burned meat filled the cabin.

"I might have known you couldn't cook, you vixen. If you burned that meat o' purpose, I'll beat the hide off you."

"Oh! Don't be hard on me, sir. Accidents will happen. I'll cook you some more, I will."

But the colonel saw through Susan's acting. "You get out o' here, and don't you show your impudent face again," he ordered. "Take the brat and the hound along with you. We were going to let you young-uns stay till your father and mother came home. But we'll have no more of your sassy tongue and your burnt victuals. Get your bonnet and get off these premises before I can count twenty. One—two—three—"

Faith sobbed. Traveler growled. But Susan was silent and held her chin in the air as she hastily grabbed some johnny-cake and maple sugar out of the cupboard and wrapped them in a cloth, took down her sunbonnet and Faith's from their hooks behind the door, untied Traveler, and marched out leading the dog by one hand and her sister by the other.

"Oh, Susan, wha-what are we go-going to do-o-oo?" sobbed the little girl.

Her sister did not answer till they were halfway across the clearing. "Don't cry, Faith," she said. "I've got a plan. The first thing we're a-going to do is saddle Blaze and git away as fast as we can. By'n by I'll tell you the rest of my plan.

"The scoundrels! The dogs! They've ruined our corn crop already," Susan exclaimed out loud, flushing scarlet with anger. There in the cornfield were the West brothers' horses cropping the tender green sprouts and trampling them under their hoofs. "I'll show them whose corn that is," she muttered as she ran to the barn for the saddle.

Holding a lump of maple sugar on her palm, she lured Blaze from her breakfast of dewy grass to the bars of the stump-lot fence. Never before had she saddled and bridled a horse so quickly. A forceful dig in the ribs from Susan's heels and a whispered, "Hurry, Blaze! Hurry!" were all that the wise horse needed to tell her that she must do her best. Traveler trotted reluctantly behind, now and then turning his head to look back. Was it his duty to stick by his mistress or to defend her home?

"It's alright, Traveler, come on." That settled the matter. The hound went bounding along ahead.

"Now, Faith," said Susan as they rode along, "will you be a good girl and stay at Joe Barnes' cabin while I take a long ride? I'll be back jest as quick as I can git there."

"I want Mother. I'm going to go to Mother," the little girl insisted.

Susan felt desperate. "Listen to me, Faith, we can't have Mother today. We mustn't bother her nor the Lathrops, when Mrs. Lathrop may be—may be—dying. Joe'll take care of you till I git back, and Traveler will stay and look after you, too."

"Where *you* going?"

"I don't know yet, but I'm a-going to find Colonel Allen if I can or somebody to drive them Yorkers off 'fore they tear our roof to pieces and stomp our corn down, mebbe. I've got to. That's why I burnt their victuals, so they wouldn't try to keep me there to cook for 'em and wouldn't suspicion I'd gone for help, if I went off."

"I'm a-going with you," announced Faith, with a stubborn expression about her small mouth.

"Do you want to let the Yorkers ruin our cabin and our crops and take our land? Do you want us to have to go and find a new home somewhere?"

The child's sunbonneted head shook a vigorous "No."

"Then, Faith, you must stay at Joe's. I've got to ride Blaze as hard as she can go it and travel light. I may be riding all day. You and I must be brave today—braver than we've ever been before."

A spark from Susan's flaming courage kindled in Faith's bosom. "I'll stay at Joe's," she said firmly, "but I do hope you'll git back 'fore dark."

Susan reached into the saddlebag, pulled out a good-sized lump of maple sugar, and pressed it into her sister's hand.

Chapter XIV

A Desperate Ride

Joe Barnes' cabin, set in a beaver meadow beside the creek, was not much bigger than a beaver house itself. The old trapper often chuckled over the fact that he had never had to make a cutting. "The little critturs" had done it for him. Susan peered anxiously through the trees to see if Joe was at home and drew a breath of relief at the sight of the thin column of smoke rising from the chimney. He was sitting on his doorstone mending a broken trap and whistling as cheerfully as the bobwhite that nested in the meadow.

Traveler bounded ahead to give notice that his mistress was coming. "Wal, I'll be switched if 'tain't the Eldredge gals!" Joe exclaimed, his face crinkling with smiles. "You must o' knowed that I was going to have rabbit stew for dinner." His little bright eyes detected in an instant that all was not well with the "Eldredge gals." "Something gone wrong over to your place?" he asked, peering up under Susan's bonnet brim.

He listened to her breathless account of what had happened, giving little sympathetic cluckings with his tongue and muttering imprecations under his breath. "The dirty varmints! The weasels! The skunks!" he raged. "They're worse'n varmints, those Yorkers. I'll bet ye a pound them's the very fellers Colonel Allen was tryin' to pick up the scent of yesterday. He come up the creek in a boat toward sundown. Said he'd heard down to Pittsford that a couple o' Yorkers and a Yorker sheriff was headed this way."

"Oh, Joe! Where did Colonel Allen go?" It seemed to the troubled girl that if she could only find the tall, homely commander of the Green Mountain Boys, everything would be alright.

Joe Barnes shook his head. "You can't never tell where Ethan Allen's going to light next no more'n where a bird will perch."

But Susan's determination to find the colonel was unshaken. "I'm going over to Paul Moore's," she said. "Sometimes he stops with him. Anyway, he may know where Colonel Allen's gone."

Joe look worried. "Don't you go gitting yourself lost, child. You don't know the roads. You'd better let me take the horse and go over there."

It would have been so much less terrifying to stay here with Faith and let Joe go. But the girl did not trust him with this mission. He would stop and talk too long on the way. If he saw a fat duck or a partridge, he would pause to shoot it. And he would give up too easily. "I can follow directions, and you can tell me how to get there," she insisted.

"'Tain't safe fer a gal to go riding around this country. You might—"

"It's safer than staying at home right now," she interrupted.

"Well, you keep on this trail till you come to a ford," he began, realizing that nothing he could say would persuade her to give up her errand.

She listened carefully to his instructions, repeated them after him, kissed Faith goodbye, gave Traveler a pat, and was off at a fast trot. Joe shook his head gloomily as he watched her disappear into the woods.

For the first time in her life, Susan was riding through the wilderness alone. All the shuddery tales she had ever heard of perilous adventures in the forest went through her mind—bear stories, wolf stories, lost girl stories. They told up here in the Grants about a woman who got off the trail on the way home from a neighbor's one day in midsummer and wasn't found till almost a year later. Then she was so nearly starved and so ragged and queer-acting people thought at first she was a crazy woman, till they found out she'd been wandering round in the depths of the woods all that time, clear up into Canada and back again, sleeping in caves and living on berries and bark and such things.

Well, if she remembered directions and kept a sharp watch for the blazes on the trees, she wouldn't get lost. As for wolves, they could find plenty to eat this time of year without bothering humans. "Hurry, Blaze! We've got to hurry, or the Yorkers will have our roof off," she murmured, patting the mare's brown neck and leaning forward in the saddle. Blaze seemed to understand that her rider was in trouble and felt responsible, just as Traveler had. Her small hoofs scarcely touched the path, so swiftly were they lifted again.

Susan's heart pounded against her ribs and Blaze snorted as three Indians on silent feet seemed to rise out of the ground ahead of her. They stopped and looked at her curiously, amazed at meeting a girl alone in the woods, then grunted friendly greeting and went on.

It was nearly noon before Blaze and her rider came to a clearing and a cabin. "No, Paul Moore don't live here," the man who was hoeing corn told Susan. "His cabin is 'bout two, mebbe three, mile north o' here. It's the next clearing."

"Have you seen anything of Colonel Allen round here this morning?" she asked eagerly.

"He was by here last night and wanted to know if I'd seen

any Yorkers. I said, 'No, and I don't want to see none neither!' If they come round here, I'll—"

Susan did not wait to hear what the man would do. She was off, urging Blaze into her fastest trot. "We're on his trail," she whispered encouragingly. To the girl's disappointment, there was no smoke coming out of the chimney of the next cabin. Her knock on the door sent a mouse scampering to his hole and started up a crow from the garden patch but roused no humankind. She had counted so heavily on the trapper's help in following up the colonel without ever taking into consideration the fact that he might not be at home. All at once, she realized that she was hungry and that her legs and back ached from sitting so long in the saddle. But she must not stop to rest. The sun was overhead now. She must get help and be home before night fell in the woods. It made her shudder even to think of being overtaken by darkness on these trails where one had to watch every marked tree to keep from getting lost.

Taking the cold johnnycake and maple sugar out of her pocket, she began munching them in alternating bites as she rode along. Once she stopped Blaze, leaned over, and held a generous morsel of sugar under her brown velvet nose. "You deserve it and more, too," she whispered. When they had gone about a half hour's ride from Paul Moore's cabin, a figure appeared in the path ahead coming toward her. As the distance between them lessened, Susan saw that it was a man of about Joe Barnes' age. He carried a rod over his shoulder and a string of fish in one hand and walked with a noticeable limp.

"Wal-l-l," he exclaimed, too amazed at meeting a girl alone in the woods to bid her good morning. "Where'd you come from, and where are you going all by yourself, young lady?"

"I'm looking for Colonel Allen, sir. Joe Barnes said he thought he was going to stay the night at Paul Moore's cabin, but there ain't nobody there, and I've got to find the colonel because the Yorkers are going to take the roof off our house and not let us live there anymore, and my father and mother and brother are all away, and there ain't nobody but me to do anything." She stopped for breath.

"I vum! You're a plucky young-un, you are. What's your name, and where's your father's pitch?"

"I'm Paul Moore," he told her when she had answered his questions. "I was jest down to the river ketching me a mess o' fish for my dinner. How many o' them Yorkers are there down to your place, and when did they land there?"

Somewhat impatient of taking time for further details, Susan began to fill in her story, while Mr. Moore punctuated it with exclamations both angry and sympathetic. "So that's where the pirates dropped anchor this morning!" He had been to sea in his younger days and still talked like a sailor, especially when he was mad. "They boarded your craft, did they, and pitched you and your little sister overboard? The black-hearted dogs. Wal, if they ain't jest a-craving for a taste o' the rope's end. And they're going to git it too, or my name ain't Moore. Pirates always come to a bad end, always."

The lame man continued to pour forth threats against the Yorkers while Susan waited, grudging every second of delay. "Please tell me where Colonel Allen's gone and when he left here." She took advantage of the fact that the trapper had stopped talking for an instant in order to spit.

"I guess he's somewhere between Bridport and New Haven 'bout now. But, lawsy-massy, at the rate he walks he might be clear to New Haven. If I had as good a pair o' legs as Ethan has, I'd join the Green Mountain Boys myself." He looked regretfully at his stiff ankle. "You weren't figgering on following him, was you?"

Susan nodded emphatically. "I must hurry too."

The trapper looked at her with a doubtful expression. "'Tain't safe for a gal to go traipsing round here alone. And it's mighty unlikely that you'd find Ethan. You don't know the shortcuts he takes or the places where he's liable to stop. Why, he has got as many holes and hiding places as a fox, and he's hunted like a fox, ever since the Yorker governor put a price on his head."

"But I've *got* to find him, or we'll lose our home," she insisted desperately.

"Well then, by Jehoshaphat, I'll go with you. You ride me back to my cabin, and I'll grab a bit o' victuals and catch my old mare, Nancy. 'Twon't take me but a minute."

Back at the cabin, Paul Moore limped briskly about, munching huge bites of bread and cold salt pork as he saddled his roan mare, slung rifle and powder horn over his shoulder, and stuck his hunting knife in his belt. Meanwhile, Susan jumped down from Blaze's back and let her rest and crop mouthfuls of green grass.

"You are very kind, sir," she said to the trapper, then remembering the string of trout, she added, "and you was going to have such a good dinner, too."

"I'd ruther help ketch Yorkers than eat any day," he said grimly.

They were off on the trail again with the roan mare taking the lead. To the girl it seemed as though a great weight had rolled off her slight shoulders. For the first time since leaving home, she relaxed in the saddle, for now she did not need to watch constantly for marked trees. Gone was that feeling of dread lest she miss the way and suddenly find herself in pathless woods. Yet she began to wonder uneasily if this were a foolish errand she had started on. Could they possibly find Colonel Allen and be back before the Yorkers had finished their dirty work and gone? Anxiously, she watched the sun.

A few miles beyond the scattered cabins that made up Bridport, Mr. Moore drew rein, sniffed the air, examined the tracks in the path, and, turning sharply into the woods, rode down to the river's edge. "Thought I smelled smoke." He pointed to the remains of a campfire. "That's where he et dinner. Them's Ethan's footprints." He was off again at a fast trot, Blaze following close to the old mare's heels. No ten-year-old was going to beat a youngster like her on the trail.

"Clumpity, clumpity, clump!" sounded the hoofs in quick time. Rabbits hopped to cover and squirrels scurried into the treetops out of sight, unseen and unheard by the two riders, whose eyes were fixed straight ahead, except when they looked to see how fast the sun was dropping toward the west.

"That Ethan! He must be bounding along like a buck," muttered the trapper. Again Susan began to wonder if her long ride was to be in vain. How her back ached, and how stiff her legs were getting! Never before had she sat so long in the saddle. Presently they rounded a sharp bend in the trail. Beside a spring that bubbled up from beneath a great rock stood a man with his rifle pointed toward the two riders. He was tall and wore gilt epaulets on his broad shoulders.

"Put up your gun, Ethan. It's Paul," shouted the trapper.

"If you want to bag two land pirates and a Yorker sheriff, turn around and come back with us lickety-split," he added as soon as they were close enough to talk to the colonel. "They've driven this gal out of her home, and she's been riding all over kingdom come trying to find you, 'fore they've torn the roof off her house, as they promised they would, and skedaddled off again."

The colonel looked up into Susan's anxious dark eyes. "Bless me," he said, "if it ain't the gal from Winfield, Connecticut—Susan—let me see—Susan Eldredge, that's it."

She was flattered that he remembered the girl he had talked to under the catamount more than a year ago. As he strode along beside Blaze, she told him all that had happened, beginning with the day last fall when the West brothers had first put in an appearance. His heavy laugh rang through the woods at her description of the fright she had given them by pretending

"Put up your gun, Ethan. It's Paul."

that he was within calling distance and again at the incident of the burned steaks.

"We'll give 'em a worse scare today than they got last fall—one they'll remember longer, the 'tarnal poltroons. So they brought along a sheriff to scare you with, did they? It's time they learned that a Yorker sheriff ain't got, and never will have, any authority in the Hampshire Grants. Tell you what we'll do, little miss; we'll stop at Cap'n Benton's in Bridport and git him to come along, and I'll borrow a horse for myself. Zeb Reed'll join us too, if he's home. Then we'll ride like the Old Boy was after us, and we'll catch the weasels if it takes all night. I've been wanting to git onto the scent of those West brothers. They've been jest asking for a taste o' the beech seal for months."

The tired girl drew strength from Ethan Allen's confidence. The sight of him swinging along, keen and tireless as a hunting dog on the trail of a fox, made her drooping shoulders straighten. He told story after story of past exploits with Yorkers, partly because he loved to brag and partly because he realized that her spirits needed the stimulus of his cheerfulness and courage.

"Did you ever hear about the time we gave a little lesson to a Dutchman in Arlington who talked too much?" he asked.

Susan shook her head.

"Old Doc Adams, he was always a-sympathizing with the Yorkers and telling the settlers they might jest as well submit to Governor Tryon and pay the big money he wanted for a new title to their land and that the Green Mountain Boys was jest a bunch o' troublemakers. So one day the Green Mountain Boys decided to pay him a visit—a surprise visit. Well, to make a long story short, we gave him a trial and sentenced him to hang in a chair under the stuffed catamount in front of o' Landlord Fay's. Then we tied the notorious old feller into one o' Fay's armchairs and hoisted him up, and there he sat while the folk stood round and told him what they thought of him."

The colonel threw back his head and laughed uproariously at the recollection. For the first time since morning, Susan laughed.

"*You* wouldn't like to sit up under that old cat, would you, Susan?"

"I should say not. He looks too much like a live one. … Aren't you ever afraid?" asked the girl presently.

"Afraid of what?" He sounded as though there wasn't a thing in the world to be frightened about.

"Oh, that somebody will seize you and take you to Albany to git that reward the governor's offered. Father says it's a hundred pounds now."

"A hundred pounds—dead or alive—that's what I'm worth. Think of that!" he chuckled. "But you see, Susan, before anybody can claim that money, he's got to ketch me. And I'm jest like one o' those grizzled old foxes that's been chased so long he knows how to fool all the hound dogs. I've had some close shaves, though. Once right over in Bridport too, at the Richardsons'.

"I stopped in there with Eli Roberts one evening to see if we could git a bite to eat and stay the night. When we walked in, who should we see sitting around the fire but twelve men from the garrison over at Crown Point. Lawsy massy! There were so many guns in that room, you could hardly step without knocking one over."

Susan gave a little gasp.

"They knew me right off, too. I could tell from the way they looked at me and then at each other. 'We've got the old fox now'—that's what those glances meant. Well, I didn't let on I suspected a thing. Called for a bowl of punch and passed it around like they were all my best friends. After supper I says to the Richardson gal, 'Have you got a bed for Eli and me?' 'Not a bed left,' says she.

"Then one o' the sergeants spoke up and offered to give up his bed and sleep in the barn. Butter wouldn't have melted in his mouth, he was so polite. 'No, no, sergeant,' says I, jest as polite as he, 'first come, first served. Eli and I'll sleep on the hay, and I guess we're ready to bed down right now.'

"The sergeant looked worried, and I could see him gitting ready to grab his gun. Then Eli and I, we took off our pistols and laid them on the table in plain sight and leaned our guns against the wall in the corner like we were putting them to bed for the night. Right away that sergeant relaxed, and so did all the rest of them. They figgered we wouldn't go off without our guns."

"Did you really go to bed?" asked Susan, too excited to wait for the rest of the story.

"Yes, siree. We went to bed in the barn, like we said we were a-going to, but we didn't stay to bed long. 'Twan't more'n half an hour 'fore we were skedaddling through the woods. 'Bout the time those soldiers decided we were sound asleep and could be captured without any trouble, we were at Shoreham knocking up Paul Moore. I'd have given a lot to have seen those fellers' faces when they marched in the barn to take us prisoners and found the barn was empty." Again the woods echoed to the colonel's laughter.

"Did you ever git your guns and pistols back?"

"Took 'em with us." He grinned at the girl's look of blank amazement. "The Richardson gal handed them out the window to us when the men weren't looking."

It seemed only a few minutes before they were in Bridport again, riding up to the door of Captain Benton's cabin. "Hey, Cap'n, saddle your horse quick as greased lightning and come with us. We've work to do," called Colonel Allen. "You'll ketch up with us. I'm a-going to borrow Ebenezer's mare if I can and call for Zeb. Happen to know if Zeb's home today?"

The tall, young captain started for his pasture on a run, calling over his shoulder, "He went duck shooting this morning, but I guess he's home now."

The sight of the three riders presently vanishing down the trail ahead on horses that were fresh and ready to trot was a pleasant sight to the girl. She and Paul Moore followed at a distance, for Blaze was too tired to hurry anymore. As they rode, Susan watched the sun and said over and over in prayer, "Let them git there in time to ketch the Yorkers!"

Chapter XV

"Nothing to Be Afeerd Of"

Joe Barnes stood in his cabin door listening to the sound of horses coming slowly down the creek in the gathering dusk. "I thank the Lord you're back agin safe, Susan. I thank God!" he exclaimed fervently as he lifted her down from the saddle. "I was fearful worried till Allen and the others come tearing by 'bout an hour ago. I hollered to him had he seen you, and he said you was coming with Paul. Was my mind relieved! I'd been kickin' myself black and blue all day for letting you go wandering off alone that way and was wondering if I hadn't ought to start out and git somebody to help me look for you. Don't know when I've been so worried."

Susan answered the trapper's greeting with the mere ghost of a smile. She couldn't speak. She could hardly stand up. Traveler, bounding joyfully to meet his mistress, nearly knocked her down.

"Now you set right in that old armchair o' mine, and we'll have a little rabbit stew," suggested Joe as soon as they were inside, for he saw at a glance how white and spent the girl looked. "Jest see that little un." He pointed to the built-in bed in the corner where Faith lay sleeping so soundly that she did not even know that Susan had come home. In the crook of her arm lay a corncob doll.

"She tagged me around all day like she was scairt she'd lose me, till finally she fair toppled over all tuckered out. Did she fret about you? Yes, she kept pestering me to know when you was coming back and if I thought you was lost. Wal, I made her that doll and told her Paul Moore would look after you, and finally she kept quiet. But, Jerusalem! I didn't know myself whether you'd find Paul or not."

The three of them sat down to steaming bowls of stew, while Faith slept on with her new doll. "My land, child, you eat like a wolf after a long, hard winter. Ain't you had any victuals all day?"

"Nothing but some johnnycake and maple sugar I took in my saddlebag," said Susan as she started in on her second bowl of stew.

It seemed as though the hot food sent waves of strength into her tired back and legs. For the first time that day, the Yorkers were forgotten. Nothing seemed to matter except that the long ride was over. Deep peace had descended upon Traveler too, with his mistress' arrival. He lay softly snoring under her feet. Home and happiness were where she was. Only when she moved from her chair did he rouse up and watch her uneasily out of half-opened eyes.

Meanwhile, Blaze rolled in the dewy grass to rub the sweat and dust from her brown coat and ate as greedily as Susan did. Now and then, she let out her breath in a long "Pr-r-r-r" of relief.

Joe and Paul Moore exchanged the gossip of Shoreham and competed with each other in telling tall tales, tales which Susan, nodding in the armchair, heard not at all. Only the drone of their voices penetrated her blissful drowsiness. She was too sleepy even to wonder if the Green Mountain Boys had caught the Yorkers and whether or not the roof was still on the cabin. Yet, the instant hoofbeats were heard outside, she was on her feet. Traveler, too, leaped up from a nap wide-awake and barking.

"Halloo!" Out of the dark came the voice of Colonel Allen. A grin stretched clear across his lean face, and his dark eyes were alight as he clumped into the cabin followed by Zeb Reed, also on a broad grin. "Well, little miss, your Yorkers are recumbent in your barn, tied hand and foot. That dog-kicking colonel has got a pretty sore back where we gave him the beech seal, but the other two are resting comfortably on a bed o' hay with the cap'n jest outside the door in case they need any attention, bless 'em."

"Did they take our roof off?" asked Susan anxiously.

"Every bit of it, and tomorrow morning at the crack of dawn they're going to begin putting it right back on again."

"And did they spoil our corn?"

"'Bout half of it the horses et off, and the rest they tromped down and rolled in, I should say from the looks of it. But before them gentlemen take their leave, I'm going to hand them a little bill for that corn that'll convince them that young corn is expensive fodder for horses."

"Had any supper?" broke in Joe, preparing to water for a second time the stew that he had expected would last him for three days.

"Supper! I should say we had—juicy bear steaks, like the ones Susan burned up this morning." He laughed a great laugh at the recollection of Susan's trick, tipped the stool he sat on back against the wall, and stretched out his long legs comfortably.

Faith, roused by the commotion, sat up, rubbed her eyes, and called, "Mother! Mother! Susan!" Finding that Susan was there, she cuddled down with her doll and was sound asleep again in a few moments.

Meanwhile, the two trappers had been waiting uneasily for

a chance to ask questions. "Tell us about the fight." "Did they put up much resistance?" "Was they surprised to see ye?" "Did you give 'em a trial?"

Ethan Allen shook on his stool till its front legs came down to the floor with a crash and set the pewter plates on the table to clattering. "Resistance! Boys, I wish you could have seen them thieves when we got there. We tied our horses in the woods and sneaked up on 'em, quiet as Indians. As we come within hearing of the cabin, we listened for voices, but there wasn't a sound. Sez I to the cap'n and Zeb, 'Bet you ten shillings they've skedaddled.' Then we saw a gleam of light shining out from the cabin. Up we crept to the winder and looked in. Lawsy massy! There lay the three of them stretched out dead drunk. The colonel, as he calls himself, had one bed, and his dear little brother had the other, and the Yorker sheriff lay right in front of the door. Guess he was supposed to be the sentry, but he was jest as drunk as the other two. We figgered that after they took the roof off, they'd sot down to celebrate with some good hot flip, and by the time they had celebrated for a while, they'd plumb forgot whether they were in Northborough or in Albany.

"They sobered off quick enough when they saw three rifles leveled at 'em. By the time we had tied their hands behind their backs and their feet together, they could set up and tell us who they were. We gave them a proper trial, found them guilty of trespass, wanton destruction of property, and disorderly conduct and sentenced them to receive thirty blows of the beech rod, to give a day's labor putting back the roof, and to pay a fine of sixteen shillings for the property they'd destroyed."

"Did you beat them very hard?" asked Susan, who hated to think of even a Yorker who was stealing her home being flogged.

"To tell the truth, Susan, we let the rabbity one and the sheriff off from that part of the punishment, but the impudent, dog-kicking colonel had to have a lesson he'd remember. And we didn't beat him so awful hard, for we wanted to be sure he'd be able to help the others put the roof back on tomorrow. It's the first real work he's ever done in his life, if I ain't greatly mistaken. Guess he'll git some blisters on those lily-white hands."

He tipped forward, rose, picked up his rifle from where he had leaned it against the wall, and slung it over his shoulder. "Come, boys," he said, turning to Paul Moore and Zeb Reed, "I suggest that we go and see how the cap'n's getting along. Guess we'll have to take turns sleeping tonight. You and the little gal, Susan, had better stay here, if Joe can take care of you, while the rest of us camp out over at your place."

"That's the very proposition I was about to make," said the trapper. "I'll lay me a bed o' hemlock boughs out under the trees and roll up in a blanket. I'd ruther sleep out there this time o' year anyhow."

The cabin seemed very quiet when the three men were gone. Again Susan's head began to nod. Joe got up, went to a wooden chest, and pulled out some homespun sheets that had not been used for years. Winter and summer, he slept on a blanket with his clothes on, as he had years before in the Indian Wars. Gentle-handed as a woman, he lifted the sleeping child, spread a sheet smoothly across the bed, put Faith down again, and tucked the upper sheet and a blanket around her. Then, having lighted the candle in the tin lantern that hung on the wall, he picked up a blanket and started for his airy bedroom. "If ye git scairt, Susan, jest holler," he told her. "I'll be near enough to hear you. But there ain't nothing to be afeerd of."

As the girl stretched out beside her sister, she realized that never before in her whole life had she been so tired. It seemed a week since her mother had called her that morning to come help milk the cows. Sleepily, she wondered how things were at the Lathrops' and where her father and Nathan were staying tonight. How strange to think of the family scattered like this and their cabin without a roof. How strange to be lying here in Joe's cabin with only Faith and Traveler for company. "There ain't nothing to be afeerd of," the old trapper had said, and with his cheerful words in her ears, she fell into a sleep that was peace itself.

Chapter XVI

Colonel West Soils His Shirt Ruffles

As they drew near home, Blaze pricked up her ears and started off at a quick trot. "Now I'm getting back to my own pasture," she seemed to be saying to herself. "Thank goodness my mistress is done with all this traipsing around." But Traveler looked worried and growled. He was thinking, "I smell the man that kicked me and was so disagreeable to my mistress. No good can come of his hanging around our place."

It was only a little after sunrise. The two girls and Joe Barnes had breakfasted at the first signs of daybreak, so eager were they to see what was going on at the Eldredge cabin. As the two girls on horseback and the man on foot rounded the last blazed tree and came into the clearing, a strange sight met their eyes. The cabin was open to the heavens except for one corner, where two perspiring men in wrinkled fine coats and dirty, torn white linen shirts worked replacing the heavy strips of bark they had ripped off the day before. Another man, the colonel's brother, mopped his brow as he dug up the cropped and trampled corn so that the field might be ready to replant.

Susan couldn't quite keep from feeling a little sorry for the Yorkers, in spite of all the fright and weariness they had caused her; they were so changed from the impudent, bullying dandies of the day before. Not one of the three raised his eyes as she and Joe called cheerful good mornings to Colonel Allen and Captain Benton, who walked up and down with their rifles over their shoulders.

"Want some breakfast?" asked the colonel, quite as though he were the host of the occasion. "Paul and Zeb have cooked some nice bacon, thanks to the forethought of our busy guests." With a mocking grin, he nodded toward the two on the roof. The girls and Joe, who had hurriedly eaten cold bean porridge, were in no mood to refuse bacon. The very smell of it floating from the doorway made them as hungry as though they had come away breakfastless.

The cabin was as changed inside as outside. The floor that Susan had carefully swept twenty-four hours before was tracked all over with muddy bootprints. The hearth was grease-soaked. Dirty, fly-laden dishes cluttered the table. Sour-smelling leather jacks stood on the floor and on the mantel shelf with dregs of flip in the bottom of them. The beds were tumbled up as only men sleeping with their clothes on can tumble them. It seemed to Susan that the house looked less like home than it had on that April morning a year ago when it had stood forlornly waiting for them.

Around the table, Paul Moore and Zeb Reed lounged, smoking their pipes and resting after their early-morning watch over the prisoners. At the sight of the two dejected girls, Paul pointed to the frying pan on the hearth. "Have some bacon. If you hadn't come quite so early, Zeb and I would have had this place tidied up a bit."

Susan washed three plates and sat down with Faith and Joe to a second breakfast. In the midst of it, she was aware of the patient lowing of the cows. "Why the poor critturs!" she exclaimed. "They haven't been milked since yesterday morning."

"Oh, yes they have," said Zeb. "The captain and I stripped

... two perspiring men ... replacing heavy strips of bark.

them last night. You don't think we missed a chance to have some warm milk with our supper, do you?"

The Eldredge farm was a busy place all that morning. After she had milked the cows and set the milk, Susan went to work with Faith's help and gave the cabin a thorough scrubbing and a tidying that made it home again. The Yorkers continued their hard labors outside under the watchful eyes of Colonel Allen, Captain Benton, and Zeb Reed. The two trappers set off for the creek, promising to bring back a mess of fish for dinner, and kept their word.

By noon, everyone was ready for the fish, which Susan fried with a scrap of bacon left from breakfast. Among those who enjoyed the meal the most were the three prisoners, who ate with the ravenous appetites of men unused to toil.

"Guess they have a little idee now," commented the colonel grimly, "what it feels like to be a settler and work to clear land and build a cabin, only to have Yorkers take it away from you. They haven't ever done anything harder in their lives than ride around on a horse. We're educating them, Susan; we're educating them."

After the dishes were done, Susan sat down to rest on the sunny doorstone while Faith played with Betsy and Joannah, the corncob doll which she had gratefully named for Joe Barnes. Susan started instinctively as she heard a horse on the trail, then decided that perhaps Paul Moore and Joe, who had set out for home together, were coming back for something.

"Halloo-oo!" There was no mistaking the voice. She knew instantly from its tone that Jonathan brought good news. His smiling eyes confirmed the cheerful "halloo." Gone was the anxious, faraway look. "She's better," he called out as the girls ran to meet him. Then his jaw dropped as he saw the two men with guns on their shoulders and the three sulky workers. "What in blazes!" he exclaimed.

"The Yorkers came and took our roof off and turned their

horses into our corn, and I rode way over beyond Bridport yesterday to find Colonel Allen, and he and Captain Benton and Zeb Reed and Paul Moore came back with me and—" At this point, she had to pause for breath. Faith snatched at the opportunity to tell her part of the tale. "I stayed at Joe Barnes', and he made me a corncob doll. I'll show her to you. Her name's Joannah, and we had bacon for breakfast."

"Jerusalem! What a time you two girls have had," broke in Jonathan. "And I thought we were gitting all the bad luck at our house. How in the world did you know where to find Colonel Allen?"

They sat down on the doorstone. "Before I talk any more," said Susan, "tell us about your mother."

"Well, she was terrible sick yesterday, but last night she didn't seem out of her head quite so bad, and this morning she knew me and said, 'Good morning, Jonathan.' Father didn't git home with Doctor Baker till most suppertime. But the doctor said your mother had done jest the right things and that she'd probably saved mother's life. She seemed to know what to do like she was a doctor herself."

"Oh, Jonathan, I'm so glad she's going to git well. I guess things are coming out all right for all of us. But yesterday it didn't seem's so anything was ever going to be the same again."

The girl and the boy talked so hard that Faith gave up the hope of having a chance to relate the adventures of herself and Joannah and went off to play.

"I didn't know there were any girls like you," said Jonathan when Susan had filled in the details of the day before. "Most girls would have cried or fainted or done something foolish, I guess." The profound admiration in his look and tone embarrassed Susan. "But wouldn't we have worried if we'd known you was wandering round the woods like that!"

Colonel Allen strolled up to the door, his eyes a-twinkle. "This is Jonathan Lathrop," said Susan.

"Ain't you proud of your girl, Jonathan?" asked the colonel. "We're going to call her Captain Susan and make her an honorary member of the Green Mountain Boys."

Susan didn't know whether she was more proud or embarrassed by his words. Anyway, she must set him right about herself and Jonathan. "I'm not his girl," she protested, her cheeks growing crimson. "He's jest a neighbor."

The dark eyes were now dancing with amusement. "I beg your pardon," he said in a teasing tone. "Jest a neighbor, is he?" Turning to Jonathan, his glance took in the boy's broad shoulders and fearless gray-blue eyes. "You look like you'd the makings of a Green Mountain Boy yourself."

Jonathan's face lighted with pleasure. "Oh, thank you, sir. I'd be proud to have that title."

"Well, we may call on you to help us chase Yorkers one o' these days. Now, Susan, your roof is on again, and your cornfield's ready for planting, and here's something to pay your father for the damages." He dropped the silver shillings one by one into her pinafore. The girl watched him, fascinated, for she had never seen such a handful of money before.

"Oh, sir!" she exclaimed, gathering the folds of her pinafore tightly together so as not to lose a shilling. "I jest never can thank you enough for all you've done for us, never."

His dark eyes that sometimes looked so stern and sometimes so bold and bragging were soft and kindly as he looked down into her face. "Little missy, I guess our accounts are jest about square. I helped you out of a tight place, and you helped me find two Yorkers I've been trailing for weeks without ever running them to cover. Now we'd better be taking ourselves and our prisoners off if we're going to see them headed for the New York line 'fore nightfall. And if ever you have any more trouble with land pirates, jest send for me, and I'll come."

The two girls and the boy stood and waved goodbye to the procession of riders setting off down the trail as long as they could see the colonel's broad-brimmed hat swinging in the air. "Father said to tell you that he'll come over and stay here tonight if you want him to, that is, if Mother ain't no worse," said Jonathan as he mounted Starface.

Susan smiled and shook her head. "I'm much obliged, but he don't need to come. Don't seem's so I'd be scairt of anything now."

The story of the coming of the Yorkers to the Eldredge cabin and of Susan's ride for help was told again and again up and down Otter Creek. Joe Barnes recounted it to everyone he met on his trap-setting and hunting trips, enlarging upon the part he played and making a taller tale with each telling. Susan described every detail of that long day to her mother, who came home two days later. Mr. Eldredge and Nathan had to hear it when they arrived on Saturday, and of course the Lathrops all wanted the story from Susan's lips.

Susan could not help taking delight in seeing how envious her brother was. "Don't see why the Yorkers couldn't ever come when I was at home," he grumbled. Mrs. Eldredge worried lest her daughter "would git too proud and conceited to live with, if folks didn't stop praising her." But Susan was in no danger of losing her head. No matter how much people called her "a brave girl," she could never forget how utterly panic-stricken, how much like running away, she had felt when the Yorkers had ridden into the yard that morning. She remembered the fear that lay at the pit of her stomach like a breathtaking weight as she had started out from Joe's cabin on the trail through the dim, lonely woods.

It seemed to her that no matter how long she lived and no matter what might happen to her, nothing could ever be quite so hard to meet again as the ordeal of that one day, when alone with little Faith she kept the Yorkers from taking possession of her cabin home.

Chapter XVII

A Peaceful Summer

The summer of 1774 was for the Eldredges one of those happy, peaceful seasons that often follow troublous times. No longer did they watch the trail uneasily or keep the rifle by the door. There was much visiting back and forth between the Eldredge and Lathrop families. Sometimes Mrs. Eldredge would ride Blaze up-creek, with Joseph in her lap and her flax wheel on the saddle in front of her, to spend the afternoon with her neighbor. Susan and Faith would follow on foot with their sewing bags, while Traveler either brought up the rear or raced ahead, dashing wildly into the woods to follow a fresh scent. What fun to have his family going places!

There were all-day working bees for the whole family occasionally, when the women and girls spun or quilted a bed quilt and the men joined forces to clear a cornfield or weeds or cut hay or have a brush-burning. At noon, the table would be lengthened to accommodate two families and heaped with food from both the Eldredge and Lathrop larders—johnnycake, bowls of samp, bean porridge, mugs of creamy milk, or maybe a kettle of steaming rabbit or a mess of fried trout, if any of the men and boys had found time to go hunting or fishing the day before.

These bees were occasions for plenty of talk as well as work. To Susan, it was always a cause for wonder that her mother and Mrs. Lathrop seemed to enjoy talking endlessly about housekeeping—patterns for butter molds, patterns for coverlets and patchwork quilts, how to set dyes. She preferred, when she got a chance, to listen in on the men as they whetted their scythes or sat under a tree resting and cooling off, and she was always ready to carry a tankard of cider or a pitcher of cool spring water to the field. Then she heard stirring tales of wolf hunts and bear hunts, of Green Mountain Boys and Yorkers, news that Amos Bosworth from Winfield was going to take up a pitch and build a cabin a little way below Joe Barnes and might be coming up any day now, rumors that Ethan Allen and other leading men of the Grants were going to petition the king to make the Hampshire Grants a separate colony with Colonel Skene as governor. The colonel owned an immense estate, called Skenesborough, at the end of Lake Champlain and held his land by a grant directly from the king.

Sometimes the young people found time from the working bee to play rollicking games of hide and seek, in which Nathan, the oldest, as well as Joseph, the youngest, liked to join. Joseph, to be sure, did little but get in the others' way and give away hiding places, but he had a wonderful time playing the game in his own way. Once in a while, Susan stayed overnight with Rachel. Then the two girls would whisper and giggle until Mrs. Lathrop called sternly, "Girls, keep quiet and go to sleep."

After that lonely first year in the woods, it seemed wonderfully good to Susan to have a girl and a boy of her own age for neighbors. Nathan seemed so grown-up now, and lately he had become too much interested in a blue-eyed girl down in Neshobe to have time for a mere sister. When Jonathan had an errand to do up-creek or down-creek, or took time to go fishing or exploring, he would sometimes ask Rachel and Susan to go with him. One day, they visited the camp some Indians had pitched for the summer about six miles up the creek. "How-do, how-do! Welcome! Welcome!" repeated the women as they fingered the bright beads the young people had brought them. Susan decided that she and her mother had easy lives, even up here in the wilderness, after she had watched these Indian women as they squatted on the shore, curing skins, cutting up a deer carcass, cleaning fish, and pounding corn into meal. And always the men were out hunting for more animals for the women to dress and cut up. Susan had to pretend she liked the raw fish the Indians offered them for refreshments, but she could hardly keep it down after she had swallowed it.

The most fun of all was the trip the three young people took to Pittsford. It was only "going to the mill," but to the two girls who stayed closely at home, it was an exciting journey out into the world. By four o'clock in the morning they were off, Jonathan and his sister on Starface and Susan following on Blaze with fat sacks of corn tied to the saddle. They ate the cold lunch they had brought with them under the trees by the millstream, where they could watch the great stone wheels turning and hear the splashing of the water. When all the shelled corn had been turned into golden meal, they packed up again and went on to the sawmill. Here Jonathan selected with care some pieces of wood and had them cut to certain lengths and turned on the lathe. What he was going to do with them he refused to tell. "I've got an idea I'll make something," he said noncommittally.

"You're going to make a table," guessed Susan.

"A chair," suggested Rachel.

"There ain't no use you girls trying to guess what I'm going to make" was all he would say on the subject.

Their last stop was at the blacksmith's shop, where Blaze had to have a new shoe to take the place of one she had lost. Fascinated, the girls watched the red-hot metal taking shape into a shoe on the anvil and then being deftly and quickly nailed by the smith onto the brown mare's dainty hoof. Blaze was much less excited about the business of being shod than was her mistress. She stood perfectly still as calmly as though nothing was happening to her. Perhaps this behavior was due to the lump of sugar—a reward for good conduct—that she could smell in Susan's pocket.

The waters of the creek were turning rosy-pink, and the thrushes were filling the woods with music as the horses jogged slowly back from the long ride. It was dusk when they turned into the trail to the Eldredge cabin. Already Mrs. Eldredge was beginning to peer anxiously out of the cabin door and was saying that she "did hope those children would git home before dark." A big kettle of bean porridge was steaming over the fire, awaiting their return. By the time the three hungry young people had eaten their fill, it was almost empty. Susan ate three bowlfuls and declared it was the best porridge she ever tasted. Her mother smiled, for she knew the supper was flavored with something she had not put into it.

Three weeks later, on the tenth of September, to be exact, Susan found out what Jonathan had made from the pieces of wood he had bought that day at the mill. In the afternoon he came riding into the clearing with a chair inverted over his head, like an enormous wooden hat. It was a beautifully made chair, with slender legs, neatly fitted ladder back, arms, and a seat woven of strips of bark. Flushed and self-conscious, he bore his work into the cabin and set it down in front of Susan. "It's for your fifteenth birthday," he said. "I sorter wanted to make you something, and it's the only thing I could think of. Mebbe you'd like a chair all your own."

Susan demonstrated that she would by sitting down in it at once and smiling a smile that began in her eyes and spread all over her face. "It's the nicest present I ever had. The nicest except Traveler," she added as the dog got up from the hearth

Susan of the Green Mountains

and began to sniff the chair with an appreciative nose. "Now I've got a chair of my very own."

Mrs. Eldredge ran her hand over the smooth wood with an admiring touch. "It's a beautiful chair," she said. "It's like one Mother gave me when Matthew and I were married. I think I hated to sell that more than any of the other furniture we had in Winfield. You were kind to go to all that trouble."

It was more trouble for Jonathan to receive thanks for his gift than it had been to make the chair. Murmuring something about having to "git right back and chop wood," he was out of the door, on Starface's back, and riding into the woods before Susan or her mother could say another word.

That evening, Susan cast stitches on her knitting needles for a pair of red mittens, promising herself that she would have them done by a certain day near the end of November. They were to have extra long wrists and a fancy border with the initials "J. F. L." knitted in colors. "I guess they'll look real pretty," she thought, "and feel good too when he's shoveling snow next winter." A smile curved the corners of her mouth as she sat in her new chair and knitted.

Chapter XVIII

The New Cabin

Puffs of blue smoke drifted across the dooryard from beyond the spring, where stumps were being burned out. The sound of axes whack-whacking their way through huge logs came from the same direction. Susan and Faith hurried through the dinner dishes, then picked up their sewing and started for the new clearing. Presently, Mrs. Eldredge, as though pulled by something she could not resist, laid down her shuttle and left the bed coverlet she was weaving on the loom to come out and "see how the menfolks were gitting along."

"It begins to look like a cabin," she said approvingly.

"Guess we'll be ready to put the roof on by tomorrow morning," Mr. Eldredge decided as he finished cutting a deep notch in the end of a log and lifted it into place with Nathan's help. Already the four log walls were more than half laid.

At his words, the girls began to sew with swifter stitches, and their mother hurried back to her loom. There was much for them to do in the short time that remained. Yes, a new cabin was going up on the Eldredge place, and everyone in the family, except Joseph, was having a part in building or furnishing it. Susan had woven and braided two rag rugs, and Faith had made a patchwork cushion. Mrs. Eldredge's gift was to be the beautiful blue-and-white bed cover now in the loom, for which she had spun and dyed the linen and woolen threads.

As soon as the wheat and corn were cut, Mr. Eldredge and Nathan had set to work felling tall, straight trees, cutting the trunks into logs of the right length, notching the ends and fitting them firmly together. There had not been so much excitement in the family before since they had come to the Grants, for Nathan was setting up an establishment of his own. Next week he was to marry pretty Deborah Warren, who had moved with her family from Winfield to Neshobe in the spring.

If Blaze could have talked, she would undoubtedly have been the first and most enthusiastic to congratulate Nathan. "Now I know," she might have said, "why you were always riding to Neshobe and why I have had to stand so many hours tied to a stump in front of that cabin. I suspected something like this all along. Maybe now I'll have a chance to stay out to pasture a little."

Joe Barnes' suspicions had also been aroused. His keen eyes were quick to notice that Nathan found frequent excuses for trips to Neshobe, and his sharp ears caught the earliest rumor wafted up Otter Creek that "Matthew Eldredge's boy was a-courting John Warren's eldest gal." "I 'spect you'll be building a new cabin pretty soon now," he remarked to Mr. Eldredge before even the first tree had been marked for cutting.

Mr. Eldredge grabbed his pipe just in time to keep it from falling out of his mouth as his jaw dropped in amazement. "How'd you know we was planning to build?"

"Wal, I figgered that Nate and his bride would live alongside of you."

"But Nate didn't ask Debby's father if he could marry Debby till yesterday!"

Joe's little dark eyes twinkled. "Guess I've lived long enough to smell a rat when it runs under my nose," he chuckled.

On a sparkling morning early in October, Nathan was up hours before daybreak, shaving his cheeks smooth by the light of a candle, brushing the dust and a cobweb or two from the three-cornered hat he had scarcely worn since he left Connecticut, and putting on his whitest, finest shirt of homespun linen and the Sunday suit with brass buttons that had grown uncomfortably tight across the shoulders.

"He didn't eat half his breakfast, he was in such a stew to git off," worried Mrs. Eldredge as the bridegroom-to-be rode away on Blaze into the red and gold woods with an empty pillion behind the saddle. "But he looks nice, anyway," she added with satisfaction. "And now, Susan, you and I have got plenty to do over in that cabin 'twixt now and tomorrow."

How they scrubbed and tidied the little new cabin! Then began a series of trips back and forth from the old house, with rugs and chairs and stools and the bed cover just off the loom. Mr. Eldredge hung the iron crane in the fireplace ready for the kettles, rolled in a backlog for the fire, and placed a basket of chips and shavings on the hearth.

Next morning, all the family were up bright and early again to make a final inspection of the cabin, put the finishing touches to their preparations for the arrival of the first bride in Northborough, and cook the welcoming dinner. "Oh! We've forgotten the candles!" exclaimed Mrs. Eldredge, just as she had about decided that the new home was ready. Then Susan recalled that she "was going to polish some of those apples Joe brought us and put them on the table."

As the morning wore on, Mrs. Eldredge and the girls fairly flew about, for no one knew how early Nathan and Deborah would come riding out of the woods. Finally, when all necessary things were done, Susan and Faith picked a great armful of purple asters and goldenrod, filled a pewter tankard with them, and set it on the doorstone. By that time, delicious smells were coming from the old cabin, and Mr. Eldredge was setting up wooden horses for a long table under the trees.

Deborah Warren had no wedding. She simply put on a bright new calico dress in place of her dark, everyday homespun and a new bonnet and rode up behind Nathan to the Justice of the Peace in Pittsford. When the simple ceremony was over, they came back to Neshobe to stay the night at the bride's home and give Blaze a rest before taking the last stage of the journey to the new home.

"Ain't she pretty, though!" whispered Mrs. Eldredge to Susan. She smiled up into the pink-cheeked, blue-eyed face under the wide-brimmed bonnet and stretched out her arms to receive her new daughter. An admiring, affectionate circle closed in around the bride as Nathan lifted her down from the brown mare's back. In that circle were not only the Eldredge family but the Lathrops young and old, Joe Barnes, and Amos Bosworth, the newest member of the little settlement along the creek who had arrived a week before to make a clearing and build a cabin for his family.

In a merry procession, they followed the bride and groom to the little cabin under the pine trees beyond the spring. How Deborah's eyes sparkled as she looked around the one room and saw all that had been done by her new family and new neighbors to make her home cheerful and attractive! On the floor were the rag rugs Susan had made, and on the built-in bed was Mrs. Eldredge's beautiful coverlet. The wooden seat of one of the stools had been softened by the patchwork cushion pieced with tiny, painstaking stitches by Faith. Across the wooden bench by the fireplace lay a tawny catamount skin, the gift of Joe Barnes. The Lathrops had brought a huge ham for the larder, and Mr. Bosworth contributed a string of speckled trout for the couple's first breakfast together. Already the cabin looked lived in, with bunches of sage and mint which Susan had gathered hanging from the rafters and the huge backlog blazing on the hearth.

In a merry procession, they followed the bride and groom to the little cabin.

After the first greetings were over, Mrs. Eldredge, Mrs. Lathrop, and the girls began dishing up food from the steaming kettles that hung over the fire in the old cabin and carrying plates, platters, and tankards to the long table under the trees. "You can call Debby and the menfolks now, Susan," said her mother as she filled a platter with roast pigeon. But they did not need to be called. The fragrance that floated across the clearing had already summoned them to posts near the table.

There was no wedding cake, but there was pumpkin pie, baked golden brown in the new chimney oven Mr. Eldredge had built that summer. They drank toast after toast to the bride and groom in long draughts of sweet cider. "Here's to the first bride in Northborough!" proposed Mr. Lathrop, raising high his tankard.

"Here's to the first bridegroom," added his wife.

"Here's to the new home! May it be a happy place!" was Mr. Bosworth's toast.

"And here's to the next bride!" shouted Joe Barnes, grinning mischievously at Susan, who to her great disgust began to blush rosy-red.

"Well, I was married when I was fifteen," said Mrs. Eldredge, "but I declare I hope Susan will wait longer than I did. I can use her at home till Faith is a lot bigger than she is now."

But Joe was unconvinced. "A gal as pretty and smart as Susan ain't a-going to stay home with her mother very long." The old trapper looked as proud as though he were talking about his own daughter, for Susan was the apple of his eye.

"You'll make the girl vain and silly," Mrs. Eldredge reproved him.

The subject of these remarks kept her eyes on her plate and was profoundly thankful when her father began to talk about Amos Bosworth's pitch.

That night when the guests were gone, the fire was banked with ashes, and the candles were all snuffed out, Susan lay in bed thinking sober thoughts. Her brother Nathan was grown up and married. That was what happened to families—they grew up and left home. In a few years she and Rachel and Jonathan wouldn't be having fun together anymore. They, too, would be "old married folks." Well, she wasn't going to think about growing up yet or about the family being split up into pieces. Anyway, she liked her new sister. That was a comfort, for she had been afraid she wouldn't. What shining eyes she had and what a merry laugh! It would be pleasant to have another cabin nearby and an older sister to come in and knit and sew with them. And next winter, when the snow again buried them alive and cut them off from all the neighbors, there would be two families on the pitch instead of one. Fixing her mind determinedly on the pleasant aspects of her brother's marriage, she fell asleep.

Chapter XIX

The Corn Husking

Outdoors, an enormous red moon was coming up over the trees. It poured a flood of light upon the clearing and made the shocks of corn stand out against the field like a regiment of fat women. Nathan and his father and Mr. Warren, who had come up from Neshobe with his wife to stay the night, needed no lanterns as they went back and forth from the cabin, carrying stools and benches and blankets. Indoors, Mrs. Eldredge, Mrs. Warren, Susan, and Debby were fairly tumbling over each other in the small space as they set out bowls heaped full of warm, crusty doughnuts and poured tankards of cider.

"Here come the Lathrops," said Susan, running to the door as the sound of a horse's hoofs was heard outside.

"Rachel and Jonathan'll be here any minute now," Mrs. Lathrop reported, taking off her bonnet and smoothing down her hair. "They can walk 'bout as fast as Starface can with Dan and me on her back." Meanwhile, Mr. Lathrop had joined the men in the cornfield.

Sure enough, in less than ten minutes the walkers appeared in the doorway, grinning at the sight of the loaded table. The next moment, loud halloos were heard from the woods as Joe Barnes and Amos Bosworth announced their arrival.

"Now everybody wrap up good; it'll git chilly out there," Mrs. Eldredge cautioned them, putting on her woolen cape and seeing to it that Susan and Faith were equally well equipped for the outdoor husking. "Did you put Traveler and Butterball out, Susan?" The girl dived under the table and pulled out the yellow cat, who clawed the floor in an effort to hold her position. She was already licking her chops in anticipation of a raid on the doughnuts. Traveler, always ready for a party, had gone on ahead to the field and was busily nosing field mice out of the corn shocks.

The company formed a laughing, chattering circle around the mountain of corn ears that lay heaped up awaiting them and began ripping the husks from the yellow kernels. It was the merriest gathering that any of them had seen since they left their homes in Connecticut. There was banter among the youngsters and talk of quilt patterns, dressmaking, and cooking on the part of the housewives. The men discussed the latest news that had been wafted up Otter Creek from New York, from Bennington, and even from farther away. Joe Barnes had seen the pamphlet Ethan Allen "writ himself and had printed down to Hartford."

"He can use as long words as a parson, he can," Joe repeated. "Puts it straight and strong too—how the rights of us settlers have been trompled on by the Yorkers and how we've been forced to take the law into our own hands 'cause we couldn't git the protection of the law from the New York Colony."

Susan, who sat on a blanket between Rachel and Jonathan, forgot for a few minutes to join in their chatter and sat silent, straining her ears to hear what the men were saying.

"Hope he sends a copy over to Governor Tryon and to them Yorker sheriffs," suggested Mr. Eldredge.

"I see an old copy of the *Hartford Courant* down to Pittsford 'tother day," reported Mr. Lathrop. "It told about that

Continental Congress they had down to Philadelphia. They said we had the right to life, liberty, and property, and no king could take our natural rights away from us. And they said the colonists was agreed not to buy any more English goods or sell anything to England."

Mr. Eldredge chuckled. "Guess that won't make much difference to us up here in the Grants. We couldn't buy anything made in England if we wanted to."

Serious talk ended in laughter. None of the little company had any idea how momentous was that decision of the Continental Congress. None of them suspected that the quarrel brewing between king and colonists would soon make the strife between Yorkers and Green Mountain Boys seem like the squabbles of children.

"All the men and boys, git ready for a husking race," announced Mr. Eldredge. "We've got to see who's the fastest husker here. When Mercy calls 'Go,' start husking as tight as you can go it, and when she says 'Stop,' everybody quit." For a few minutes after Mrs. Eldredge's signal, no sounds were heard in the field but the sharp ripping of the dry husks and the thuds of dropping ears of corn. The women and girls sat on the edges of their stools, each hoping that her favorite would be the winner. There was silence for a moment after Mrs. Eldredge called "Stop." Then each husker began counting his own pile. To Susan's delight, the red woolen cap she had knitted for the prize went to Jonathan, the youngest in the race. She had so hoped he would be the winner, for the cap matched the mittens she was going to give him next month.

There was no more excitement until Nathan turned up the first red ear and claimed a kiss from Debby. "That's what I call a waste of corn," said Joe Barnes disgustedly. "What's a married feller want a red ear for?" Sometime afterward, anyone watching the trapper closely might have seen him start to strip the husks from an ear, then pull them back over the kernels and stealthily slide the ear over convenient to Jonathan's hand.

"Red ear!" shouted the boy a moment later, and before Susan had time to duck or run, he had grabbed her and kissed her. She was thankful that it was night so that no one could see how red were her cheeks. "There," exclaimed Joe with great satisfaction, "that one wa'n't wasted."

Presently their voices rang out in the strains of the old songs they all knew. Mr. Eldredge struck up in his heavy bass:

"Two lofty ships that from ol' England sailed."

One by one, the others joined in. Then Mrs. Eldredge and Susan began to sing:

"A story, a story, a story of one,
'Twas of a great prince, his name was King John.
He was a man, and man of great might.
He tore down great barns and set up great right."

The whole circle took up the chorus, singing lustily:

"To my derry I down,
Oh, high down derry day.
Derry, derry day."

As the voices of the huskers went echoing through the forest, the wild creatures fled up-creek and down-creek, wondering what could be going on in the clearing. Was a bear hunt or wolf hunt on foot?

The mountain of corn shrunk to the size of an anthill before the attack of so many hands, and while the moon was still high overhead, the evening's work was done. Then the company trooped across the clearing to the cabin for the really important business of a husking bee. As they opened the cabin door, an aroma greeted them like the combined fragrances of an apple orchard and a well-filled pantry on baking day. "Jehoshaphat!" roared Joe. "If I don't smell doughnuts."

"It's the first time I've had my teeth in a doughnut since I came to the Grants," mumbled Mr. Lathrop, with his mouth full of one off the top of the bowl. Mrs. Eldredge beamed her appreciation. She had been saving for months to get fat enough to fry these crusty delicacies for the huskers.

Talk grew merry as the doughnuts melted away and the tankards of amber-colored cider were emptied. Joe Barnes' tales grew taller and taller the longer he ate and drank. The other men let their pipes go out trying to beat Joe at his own trade, but he could cap any yarn with a bigger one. Meanwhile, Rachel, Susan, Faith, and Jonathan played checkers and fox and geese on the hearth with red and yellow kernels of corn. Before the party showed signs of breaking up, Joseph was asleep in the trundle bed and Faith was having difficulty keeping her eyes from going shut every few minutes.

Goodbyes were prolonged. Everyone had a message to send back to Winfield by Amos Bosworth, who was starting home the next day to stay till spring, when he would come back with his family. "Good luck to you till we meet again." "Tell Grandma and Grandpa Ames that all is well with us." "We'll see that the Yorkers don't take your pitch away from you while you're gone." "Give our love to Aunt Augusta." "Tell 'Lijah Frost he'd better come and make a pitch on the creek 'fore the best land's all took." "Goodbye and God bless you." Amos was fairly loaded down with messages and good wishes.

Laughing and talking as they went, the little procession of homegoing guests started along the trail, the light of their lanterns shining through the trees after they were out of sight. The first husking on the Eldredge pitch was over.

Chapter XX

Spring of '75

Susan patted down the brown earth over the sweet-pea seeds she had just dropped in a circle around a stump, then gave them a generous drink of water from a pitcher while a gleeful brown thrasher in the tree overhead seemed to be singing:

> "Hurry up! Hurry up!
> Plant it, plant it.
> Let it grow. Let it grow.
> Hey diddle dee dee!"

She had sown more flower seeds this spring than ever before, just as her father and Nathan had sown more wheat and planted more corn. Straightening up, she looked about the yard with pleasant anticipation in her face. The hollyhocks had spread till their ranks stretched from the cabin door around the corner of the house and halfway along the side. The rose-bush Mrs. Lathrop had brought them from her own garden in Connecticut would be covered with soft pink blossoms this summer. If the sweet peas all came up, every black stump left in the yard would be beautiful instead of ugly. There were going to be mignonette and bleeding hearts too.

Again the clearing was carpeted with new grass and vio-

Susan of the Green Mountains

lets, and the trees were leafing out. Susan stood in the sunlight for a few moments, letting its warmth soak into her, just as Blaze and the cows and sheep were doing out in the pasture. She was as happy as that brown bird, and he was so bursting with joy he could not keep quiet more than a few seconds at a time.

Her father seemed to be in a cheerful mood too. She could hear his heavy bass as he sang in time to his swinging hoe the old song his father and grandfather had sung long ago as they worked their fields in England:

> *"Oh! Sometimes I harrow and sometimes I sow,*
> *And sometimes to ditching and hedging I go,*
> *No work comes amiss, I plant and I plow,*
> *I get all my bread by the sweat of my brow."*

This, the girl decided, was going to be the nicest summer the Eldredges had had since they came up from Connecticut. For the time being anyway, the Yorkers were leaving them in peace. No longer did they feel hemmed in by the dark woods, for a wide, sunny clearing surrounded the two cabins. Susan was never lonely now. There was Debby running back and forth from her cabin beyond the spring. The Lathrops and Joe Barnes made frequent visits, and below Joe's cabin the Bosworth family, eight strong, had come to join the little settlement. Any day now Ezra Lyons might arrive from Winfield to begin clearing land for his cabin. That would make eight families in Northborough, not counting Bill Bassett, a trapper who had built a shack back under Wolf Hill and never had a word to say to anyone.

She smiled contentedly. Yes, these two years of loneliness and discouragement and backbreaking work had been worthwhile after all. What was the passage from the Bible her father had read to them last night? "The wilderness and solitary place shall be glad for them, and the desert shall rejoice and blossom as the rose." That was it. "The wilderness shall be glad for them." She repeated the words over to herself. Perhaps this wilderness on Otter Creek was glad that they had come.

"Where's your father, child?" Susan started and looked up to see Mr. Lathrop standing in front of her. She had not heard his footsteps, so absorbed had she been by her own pleasant thoughts.

"He's over there beyond the spring. Want me to go git him?"

Without another word, Mr. Lathrop strode quickly across the clearing in the direction Susan's finger had pointed. He scarcely seemed to have heard what she said. "What's the matter now?" the girl asked herself, scenting trouble, and started after him on a run. She forgot she had promised her mother that she would do the churning, forgot everything except the look of excitement in Mr. Lathrop's eyes and the queer, jerky tones of his voice. Was Mrs. Lathrop sick again? She *must* know what had happened.

"Matthew!" he called out as soon as he was within hailing distance of Susan's father. "Have you heard what's happened?"

"No. Have some o' them thieves grabbed your pitch?"

"There's been a fight," panted Mr. Lathrop, for he had run more than he had walked on the way down-creek.

"Well, I hope the Yorkers got the worst of it."

"The Yorkers didn't have anything to do with this fight. It was—"

"Oh!" There was a deep relief in Mr. Eldredge's voice. "You had me scared for a minute, Dan'l. I thought them land-grabbers were up on Otter Creek again." He could scarcely see why anyone should get excited over a fight that the Yorkers had nothing to do with.

"It's worse'n that, worse'n that, Matthew. There's been a terrible fight down Boston way between the people and the king's troops."

"There's been a fight."

The basket of corn Mr. Eldredge was holding dropped out of his hand, and half the yellow kernels spilled onto the ground. "Has it come to that!" he exclaimed, not even noticing the upset basket.

For some time the people up here in the North had heard rumblings from the Massachusetts Bay Colony, and when the port of Boston had been declared closed by the king, feelings had run high. Yet they were too remote from the scene of the storm to realize what black war clouds had been gathering.

"Have ye heard about the fight down to Lexington and Concord?" It was Joe Barnes shouting as he hurried across the clearing, hoping to be the first to bring the news. Great was his disappointment to find that Mr. Lathrop had beaten him as a news-bearer by about five minutes. However, he lost no time in taking up the tale his neighbor had begun, and there followed a lively talking contest between the two men.

"It was a bloody business, a bloody business; nearly three hundred o' them redcoats ran jest like dogs with their tongues hanging out most of the way from Concord back to Boston. I guess they know now them farmers down there in Massachusetts can fight, once they git their dander up. Why, they gathered in Concord from miles and miles around when they heard Gage was sending troops out there."

"You forgot to tell about Paul Revere," broke in Joe, who had listened as long as he could without bursting from the strain. "You see, a feller named Revere from Boston, he rode all night warning folks about what was going to happen."

"For the land's sakes!" exclaimed Mr. Eldredge disgustedly. "Will one of ye begin at the beginning and tell what happened? I can't make head nor tail out of it when you keep interrupting each other. What in blazes did General Gage send troops to Concord for? And what do they mean by shooting folks? And when did this all happen, anyway? Now Dan'l, start over again, and Joe, you wait till he gits through. Then you can talk. And let's all sit down on the grass here."

"Well," began Mr. Lathrop with a gleam of triumph in his eye, "it seems the Massachusetts folks had stores o' gunpowder and lead and so on in Concord, and General Gage he—"

"Susan! Susan!" Mrs. Eldredge's call rang out clear and insistent from the cabin door.

Susan, who had been sitting as silent as one of the fence posts, her eyes twice their natural size, took as long in getting to her feet as if she were eighty years old and crippled with rheumatism. Slowly, listening as she walked, she started for the cabin. Why did Mother have to call at just that moment? Why couldn't the churning wait at least five minutes longer?

As it turned out, the cream was not churned that day. Neither was the corn planted. The crows stuffed their crops to the bursting point with the spilled kernels that Mr. Eldredge forgot to pick up. Mr. Lathrop and Joe Barnes had to tell the story of the battle of Lexington and Concord three times—first on the edge of the cornfield, again to Susan and her mother, and still again to Nathan and Debby on the doorstep of their cabin.

Mrs. Eldredge forgot to cook any dinner until Joseph reminded her that he was "awful hungry." "Goodness gracious! Sakes alive! It's long past dinnertime, and I haven't cooked a thing," she exclaimed. "It's lucky I've got a kettle of bean porridge I can warm up. You men had better sit down and eat with us." She turned to the visitors as she spoke. "There's plenty of it such as 'tis, and it's good what there is of it, as my mother used to say," she added with a laugh.

The sun crept down toward the tops of the trees while the little group sat around the table and talked, unconscious of the passing of the hours. "Looks like Massachusetts folks were in for a lot o' trouble—a lot o' trouble," prophesied Joe. "Right now I wouldn't swap my little old cabin on Otter Creek for the finest house in Boston, no-siree. Might's well live in a hornet's nest and be done with it."

Mr. Eldredge puffed thoughtfully on his pipe. "It ain't our fight," he said as though he were thinking out loud. "We've got no quarrel with the king. He's treated us a 'tarnal sight better than our own neighbors in New York have. Yet I wonder if we can keep out of it. Fighting spreads faster'n a brush fire once it gits started, and this one's been a-smoldering kinder under cover for a long time."

"Jehoshaphat!" exploded Joe. "We'll be derned fools if we git into it. We've troubles enough of our own with the Yorkers."

Mr. Lathrop, who had been sitting silent for some time, solemnly took his pipe out of his mouth. "If this fire spreads all over the Colonies like you think it's going to, Matthew, we're in a bad position here, near's we are to Fort Ticonderoga and the fort at Crown Point. The lake will be full o' troop ships, and the Indians'll come pouring down from Canady again, more'n likely."

Again Joe became explosive. "Indians! Indians! Don't set there, Dan'l Lathrop, and tell us we've got to fight them all over again. By the great horn spoon! I've done all the Indian fighting I want to do."

As Joe's spluttering ended, a step was heard on the doorstone. It was Jonathan. But it was not the laughing boy who played with Rachel and Susan. He seemed suddenly grown-up, grave, and manly. "Amos Bosworth's just back from Pittsford," he announced. "He says Colonel Allen is in Bennington holding a council of war with Captain Warner, Remember Baker, and the others and is going to send out a call for the Green Mountain Boys to drill and git ready."

Joe spit violently into the fireplace. "Jehoshaphat!" was all he could say.

"Father," said Jonathan, "I'm going to join the Green Mountain Boys."

Something like an electric shock passed from one to another of the little group. It was as though lightning that had been flashing along the horizon had suddenly struck the cabin roof. Mr. Lathrop jumped to his feet. "Now look here, Jonathan, don't you git excited and go off half-cocked. There ain't going to be any fighting up here, and if there is, you're too young to git into it." He began pacing nervously back and forth across the floor.

"I'm going on seventeen, and I can swing an axe jest as fast and aim a rifle jest as sure as any man."

Daniel Lathrop looked at his tall, broad-shouldered son. He was as straight and as strong as a sturdy wilderness tree. There was self-reliance and courage in the glance of his level gray eyes and in the firm set of his mouth. "I guess they'll take you all right," he said after a long silence, then repeated doggedly, as if trying to convince himself, "but there ain't going to be any fighting."

At Jonathan's announcement, Susan felt a sudden chill in the warm room. A cold stone seemed to be lying in her stomach just as it had the day the Yorkers rode out of the woods. Jonathan was going to join the Green Mountain Boys! If there was fighting along Otter Creek or if there was fighting in the Green Mountains, he would be in it. He might be shot down, just as those men had been shot on Lexington Green and at Concord Bridge. She had seen a deer, at one moment alive, bright-eyed, bounding through the woods, then the next moment lying motionless on the ground with dull eyes. That was what had happened to those Massachusetts farmers. That might happen to the boy she had played with ever since she could remember anything. Gruesome stories of the Indian Wars she had heard told by her father and Joe Barnes came back to her mind.

When Jonathan and his father were gone, Susan went and sat alone in her favorite place, the rock under the pine trees. But the soft murmuring of the pines could not banish her troubled thoughts. Neither could the robin singing joyously to his mate. How everything had changed since morning! Now she did not care whether the sweet peas came up or not or whether her rosebush had a single blossom. Traveler barked coaxingly, asking her as plainly as he could to throw a stick for him to chase, but she did not hear him.

At supper, Susan's father noticed how grave she was and how little she was eating. "There ain't no sense in us folks way up here gitting worried over that fracas down in Massachusetts," he said reassuringly. "It'll probably all blow over."

"You don't think," asked Susan eagerly, "that the Green Mountain Boys will have to do any fighting?"

"No, child, I don't, but they'll have a lot o' fun drilling and strutting around and telling what they're going to do when the king's troops come up here."

The girl drew a long sigh of relief. That flat taste was gone from her hasty pudding. She was sure that her father knew better than anyone else what was going to happen. Fortunately for her peace of mind, she did not realize that he felt far less certain about the future than his cheerful talk sounded.

Chapter XXI

A Secret That Couldn't Be Kept

"Can you keep a secret?"

"Have I ever told one of your secrets yet?"

Jonathan shook his head emphatically. "No, Susan. You're better than any girl I ever knew about keeping your mouth shut. But this is more important than anything I ever told you before. Father and Mother don't even know about it yet. 'Tanyrate, it ain't my secret; it's the Green Mountain Boys' secret."

Susan looked properly impressed. The boy spoke in whispers, as if afraid the trees might spread the story or that the thrush that sat looking intently at them with first one inquisitive eye and then the other might fly down-creek with it.

"Well," he began, looking carefully around, "Colonel Allen has asked all the Green Mountain Boys to be ready to march on Old Ti when he sounds the call. We're going to make a surprise attack most any night now, I guess, and they're a-going to post guards on all the roads so that no one can git word to the fort about our plans or send reinforcements over there or anything. I joined the Green Mountain Boys jest in time.

"Why, Susan, what's the matter?" He stopped short as he saw how the girl was shivering in the warm May sunshine.

"I'm cold," she said, jumping up suddenly. "Let's walk down to the creek and back."

"Cold! Land's sakes! You haven't got the ague, have you? Mrs. Bosworth's been having it bad."

"No, but maybe I've caught a cold." Not for all the world would she tell him that she was shivering at the thought of the old gray fort at Ticonderoga and the row of cannons pointing down threateningly at anyone who dared climb to its gates. She had never seen "Old Ti," but she had heard Joe Barnes tell how it crouched up there above the lake. She could see in imagination the "Old Sow," an enormous, fat-bellied mortar that might be heard for miles around when it thundered a salute. How could they be sure it would be a surprise attack? That old fort was like an owl, she was sure; it could see in the night.

Jonathan talked on eagerly in a half whisper as they walked through the woods, all unconscious of the cold fear his words were bringing to the girl beside him. "There's a lot o' gunpowder and cannon balls over there that we'll need if we have a war."

"But you don't think there's really going to be a *war*, do you?"

Jonathan shook his head. "Nobody knows what to think, but they say all the Colonies are getting ready for the worst. They're drilling over in New Hampshire and down in Connecticut."

Susan shivered again, but this time Jonathan was too busy talking to notice it. Back and forth along the woods trail they walked. The boy's eyes shone as he talked of the adventure ahead of him, but the girl's eyes were grave. All at once, Jonathan saw that the sun was shining straight down upon them and that their slim bodies cast no shadows on the mossy ground.

"Why, it's dinnertime," he exclaimed, amazed that the morning was so quickly gone. "Mother'll be wondering whatever's become o' me. Now don't forget that what I've been telling you is a secret."

Susan watched him for a moment as he went striding down the sunlit forest path, whistling lightheartedly. Then she turned and walked slowly home. Her shoulders drooped as though she were tired.

"Don't you feel well, child?" asked Mrs. Eldredge that evening as she noticed how tired and listless Susan was.

"What did you say, Mother?" The girl roused herself from her thoughts with an effort and realized that her mother had laid down her knitting and was looking anxiously into her face.

"Let me see your tongue." Susan obediently stuck out a perfectly healthy-looking tongue. "It looks alright, and you don't seem to have any fever," added Mrs. Eldredge, placing her hand on her daughter's forehead. "Are you chilly?"

"No—yes. Oh, Mother, I'm alright."

"There's a lot of fever 'n' ague around now," her mother murmured apprehensively half to herself, then got up and shut the door, as though the soft breeze of the May night might waft in the dreaded ailment.

It seemed hard to Susan that she could not tell Jonathan's secret even to her mother. Mother had an almost magical way of calming one's fears. Picking up the half-knitted stocking that lay in her lap, she began knitting and purling at a furious speed. In an effort to keep from thinking about Jonathan, she chattered about little things—the nest the phoebes had built under the eaves of the barn, the honeysuckle buds she had found in the woods, the woodchuck Traveler had almost caught. Presently the sock again lay in her lap, and her thoughts were miles away at Old Ti. Now her curly dark head was beginning to nod, and her body sagged down in the chair Jonathan had made for her.

A tall, broad figure loomed up in the cabin, stooping a little to avoid bumping the rafters. It was a familiar figure. Dark, laughing eyes looked down at the crumpled-up girl in the chair, and a smile dented the brown, leathery cheeks. "Don't you worry, little miss." His confident voice seemed to fill the whole cabin. "We'll smoke the hornets out o' that old fort without any trouble at all or my name ain't Ethan Allen."

"Oh, sir—"

"Susan! Wake up and go to bed before you fall into the fire."

"Yes, sir—er—yes, Mother," Susan corrected herself hastily as she blinked up into the face of Mrs. Eldredge. Wonderingly, she looked around the room. It took fully a minute for her to realize that the laughing-eyed colonel of the Green Mountain Boys was not there and had not been there at all. Yet, when she was undressed and had nestled down into her cornhusk bed, she felt strangely comforted. It seemed as though Ethan Allen had actually come and spoken to her and given her a little of his own never-failing courage and confidence. Her sleep was dreamless and peaceful.

Susan did not have to keep her secret long. In a few days, nothing was being talked about in the Eldredge and Lathrop cabins but the attack that was going to be made on Old Ti. Grass and weeds grew among the corn sprouts while the men discussed all the rumors that every wind seemed to blow up the creek. Men had come to Bennington from Massachusetts and Connecticut to talk over plans for capturing the fort with Colonel Allen. "Guess folks are finding out that Ethan ain't jest a lawless mob leader, like the Yorkers claim he is, but he's a man to be trusted with responsibility," said Mr. Eldredge with pride. "If we take Ti, the Continental Congress ought to declare us a separate colony, that's what they ought to do. With that fort, we can keep the Britishers off Lake Champlain and stop the Indians and the Canadians from coming down to join the fighting."

Joe shook his head gloomily. "I wouldn't feel so sure we was going to take Ti, if I was you. I hear they've got reinforcements over there."

"Who said so?" demanded Mr. Lathrop. His face grew pale under its heavy coat of tan.

Susan felt that cold lump in her stomach again. She sat on the edge of the group of men so silently no one noticed she was there. Yet she missed not a word of what was said.

"You can't believe everything you hear these days," said Mr. Eldredge soothingly.

Mr. Lathrop did not seem to hear him. "I dassn't tell Abby that. She don't sleep much of any these nights. She's so worried 'bout Jonathan's going over there. He seems like a little boy to her, even if he is pretty nigh man-grown." It was evident from the look in his eyes that he too thought of his oldest child as a "little boy."

"Yes, I know," sympathized his neighbor. "Nathan thinks he's going to join the Green Mountain Boys too."

That night, Mrs. Eldredge dosed her older daughter with some bitter herb tea that the girl could hardly swallow, in spite of Susan's protests that she was not "fixing to git the ague." "Your color's bad, and you don't act like yourself," said her mother.

Susan gulped down the hated dose. She preferred drinking the tea to explaining that she was not sick but worried—worried about Jonathan. Her mother just couldn't understand how she felt, for to her she was still just a little girl.

Chapter XXII

Susan Does Some Eavesdropping

Mrs. Eldredge carefully inspected the row of pies on the cupboard shelf, picked out one that was just the right shade of golden brown, set it into a basket, and covered it with a clean linen cloth.

"There, Susan, I wish you'd take this down to Mary Bosworth. I don't s'pose she's tasted a pie since she left Winfield. Maybe," she added with a laugh, "a piece of pie is what she needs to cure her ague."

Susan lost no time in putting on her sunbonnet, slipping the handle of the basket over her arm, and starting out. She was always glad to go visiting, but especially so today. Perhaps she would hear some news. That report Joe had brought last night about reinforcements at Fort Ti worried her. What if the Green Mountain Boys should find the troops at the garrison waiting for an attack and ready to pour a shower of bullets down onto them from the walls?

Oh, well, Joe was always hearing or imagining things that weren't so. He was sure that Bill Bassett, the grumpy trapper who lived at the foot of Wolf Hill, was really a Yorker spy, surveying for New York land-grabbers. He said he'd seen a man that looked like Colonel West go sneaking over that way a few weeks ago. Yet nobody else had seen the hated colonel in these parts since Ethan Allen escorted him down Otter Creek.

The trail that led to Wolf Hill was scarcely noticeable, so seldom was it traveled. Only by watching for a blazed tree could one tell where it branched off between Joe's cabin and the trail to the Eldredge pitch. Susan would have passed the marker this morning without seeing it had not Traveler suddenly sniffed the air and growled deep down in his throat. "It takes a bear or an Indian to make Traveler growl like that," thought Susan. Anxiously, she looked in the direction the dog's nose pointed and saw a man disappearing among the trees. He was no Indian, but she could not tell from that fleeting glimpse whether he was stranger or neighbor.

"Come, Traveler," she called as she started on. The dog stood rooted to the spot.

"Come on," she called again more firmly, after she had gone a few yards. Traveler did not budge. She whistled. His legs seemed as firmly planted in that spot as the roots of the forest trees.

What ailed the dog, anyway? Well, she would go the rest of the way without him. But, as she started down-creek again, Traveler's worried growl followed her.

"I wish I could read his thoughts," she said to herself, then stopped and walked back to the blazed tree.

"*What* are you trying to tell me?" she asked, patting his head. For answer, he started into the woods toward Wolf Hill, stopped, looked around at her, and whined. This time there was no doubt about what Traveler wanted to do. He was saying as plainly as he possibly could in his own language that they must follow that man.

Afterward, Susan wondered why she plunged into those lonely woods that morning, in pursuit of an unknown man. It was not just because Traveler was so insistent. As she looked along the dark trail, something seemed to pull her in the direction of Wolf Hill. She must find out what was going on over there. If the girl had given herself time to think, she would have realized what an utterly mad expedition it was. But she didn't think. She merely followed her instinct and her dog.

Holding Traveler firmly by the collar and warning him to "keep quiet," she hurried along, watching closely for blazes but keeping to one side of the trail so that the man ahead should not discover her if he stopped and looked around. The woods grew darker and more silent. Only an occasional bird chirped. Susan was frightened. She wanted to turn back. Yet something stronger than fear pulled her toward Wolf Hill.

When she had been walking nearly an hour, the solid ranks of pines and hemlocks suddenly opened up ahead of her. There on the back of a rushing stream was a bark hut. The girl peered out from behind the broad trunk of an ancient tree. Evidently the trapper was at home, for smoke was pouring out of a hole in the roof. As she watched, a man in a buckskin hunting suit walked up to the door, cast a quick, stealthy glance over his shoulder, knocked, and entered. Who was it? Traveler gave a muffled growl that seemed to say, "I know him."

"Now, Traveler," whispered Susan, looking straight into his understanding eyes, "don't you dare make another sound, or we're lost." Placing each foot noiselessly on the ground, careful lest a twig snap, she edged her way around the clearing and crawled into a clump of alder bushes growing close to the rear of the cabin. There she crouched and listened, never loosing her tight hold on the dog. A man's voice came through the bark wall. Susan recognized it at once as the harsh voice that had ordered her out of her own cabin a year before.

"That's right," he was saying, "now sew the lining back. Guess nobody'll find it there."

"Lining of what?" Susan wondered.

"Remember, Bill, if anybody wants to know where you're going, you're not going anywhere—just out hunting. Understand?"

Susan of the Green Mountains

A grunt was the only answer.

"When you get there, you're to put the letter *into the commander's hand*. Don't let anybody take it to him for you. Now do you remember the way I told you to go and where I said the dugout was hidden on the lake?"

There was another affirmative grunt.

"And, for heaven's sake, don't go near the Crown Point Road. It's sure to be guarded by the Green Mountain Boys. If things go wrong and the letter's found, you don't know who wrote it. You don't even know the name of the man that gave it to you. Remember that."

At this point, Bill apparently found his tongue and remarked that "it wa'n't likely anybody'd rip off his old fur cap," thus satisfying the eavesdropper's curiosity. So the letter was in his cap, was it?

"Not likely, but I want you to be prepared for anything."

Now the sound of clinking coins being transferred from one pocket to another was heard. "Wait till I've gone a while before you start," was the colonel's parting order. The door opened and slammed shut again. Four bright eyes watched from the alders as the visitor hurried into the woods. If she hadn't recognized his voice, Susan would never have known this bearded, buckskin-clad woodsman for the clean-shaven, beruffled colonel. "He's trying to look like a trapper instead of a Yorker," she decided. A rumbling sound was heard in Traveler's throat. At the sight of a warning finger pointed at him, the dog swallowed the beginning of a growl.

Stealthily, the girl crept out of the alders to the shelter of the deep woods, thinking hard as she retreated. A letter sewed up in his cap—nobody was to know who sent it—for the commander—a dugout hidden on the shores of the lake. It was a plot to warn the commander at Old Ti! There couldn't be any doubt about that. Colonel West had somehow heard that the Green Mountain Boys were getting ready.

What *could* she do? Bill Bassett had to be stopped. But a girl and a dog couldn't hold up a man with a gun. She'd go after Joe Barnes. Perhaps he could do something. She'd have to be quick about it, too.

Again she was hurrying through the dim woods. Again she was being careful to keep out of sight of the man ahead of her. The trail seemed twice as long as it had before. Would she ever get to Joe's cabin? Shivers slid up and down her spine at the thought of how much might depend on what she did this morning. At last, to her great relief, silvery patches of water shone through the woods. Almost there!

The door of Joe's cabin was tight shut. His dugout was gone from the river bank. The trapper was nowhere in sight. Even before she knocked and walked in, the girl knew that her plan was wrecked. If she went home or on to the Bosworths', Bill Bassett would be across Otter Creek and well on his way to the lake by the time they were back at the beginning of the Wolf Hill Trail.

"Joe-oe, Joe-oe!" she called desperately from the doorway, though she knew there would be no answer. As she turned around, her eyes lighted on the trapper's rifle hanging above the fireplace. She took it down. Yes, it was loaded. And she could use a gun, if she had to. Wasn't she as good a rabbit hunter as Jonathan?

What in the world was she thinking of! A girl, even if she could shoot, was no match for a man with a gun. She might as well go on home. And let Bill take that letter to the fort? Oh! Wasn't there something she could do? Her glance fell on Joe's muskrat cap and old deerskin jacket, hanging on a peg behind the door. In an instant, she had torn off her sunbonnet and pulled the cap down to her eyebrows. In another instant the trapper's hunting jacket hung in loose folds from her slender shoulders, like a scarecrow's coat.

"Come on, Traveler," she said with grim determination, "you and I have got to tend to this business alone."

Susan of the Green Mountains

Behind a clump of young hemlocks just beyond the blazed tree, the girl and the dog waited and watched the trail from Wolf Hill.

***

The Eldredges sat down to dinner without Susan. "A child that don't know enough to be home when it's time to eat don't deserve any victuals," declared Mr. Eldredge.

His wife looked worried. "Never knew her not to come right back when I told her to. 'Tain't a bit like her to stay to the Bosworths' for dinner."

By the time Mr. Eldredge had finished eating and gone out to the cornfield, he too was uneasy. The smoke from his midday pipe came in quick, nervous puffs, and he kept walking to the edge of the field and peering into the woods. "If she ain't here by the time I git two more rows hoed, I'm going after her," he finally decided.

Indoors, Susan's mother washed the dinner dishes and sat down to her spinning. The line between her eyes became a deep furrow as she worked. "'Tain't like Susan," she kept thinking.

Joe Barnes' reliable clock—the sun—marked a few minutes past noon when the trapper pulled his dugout ashore. He picked up a string of trout, shouldered his fishing rod, walked up the slope to the cabin, and kicked open the door. The first thing he saw was Mrs. Eldredge's pie basket on the table. "Must have had comp'ny," he decided. At the sight of the brown, flaky crust within the basket, his bright eyes twinkled. "By the great horn spoon! Won't that taste good with them trout! Bet a shilling it's one o' Mercy Eldredge's pies," he exclaimed out loud.

"Hul-l-lo!" The sunbonnet that lay on the floor just where it had dropped caught his eye. "Is that gal hiding somewhere to see how I like the pie?" he thought, chuckling to himself. "I'll take a look around." She was not behind the door or behind the chimney or in the shed. Oh, well, she'd come out when she got good and ready.

He poked the fire and put on fresh wood. The empty place where the rifle should have been lying met his eye. What in blazes was Susan doing with his gun! That was carrying a joke too far. He did not notice the empty peg where his hat and jacket should have been hanging.

"Susan! Susan!" he called from the doorway. "Where are you? What are you monkeying with my rifle for?"

The echo of his own voice from across the creek was the only answer.

Feeling more and more uneasy, he browned the trout over the coals and sat down to his dinner. There was something queer about this.

If that girl hadn't appeared by the time he'd finished eating, he was going up to the Eldredges'.

***

For some time after his visitor had left, Bill Bassett puttered about in the shack. He had no stomach for the errand he had to do and wished with all his heart he had never promised to undertake it. Too risky. It was one thing to do a little eavesdropping and tale-bearing for the colonel. But to carry a letter over to that fort with guards on the roads, that was different. Oh, very different! You never knew when or where a Green Mountain Boy might pop up in these woods. Once he had seen a Yorker flogged by some of those "Boys" and he would never forget it. They'd flog him plenty if they found that letter. Well, who would think of ripping up his cap? For that matter, nobody knew there was a letter but him and the colonel. He clinked the bright shillings in his pocket. The sound reassured him. There were more coming to him too, when the job was done. The thought of all he could do with the money was the only thing that kept him from backing out—the only thing, that is, except the terrible wrath of Colonel West. "Between two fires," he thought, "that's where I am."

He swore aloud as the powder horn he was filling dropped from his nervous fingers onto the dirt floor and spilled half its contents. What a butterfingers! He wasn't well. Yes, that was the trouble. Wasn't fit to go. Taking a jug from the mantle shelf, he poured a long draught of rum down his throat, then another. There, that was better. Maybe he could go now. His hand shook when he closed the door. His feet dragged slowly along the trail.

"Drop that gun! We've both got you covered." If a piece of the sky had fallen on his head, Bill could hardly have been more startled. He could not see the slim figure of the girl or her scared, white face. He saw only a muskrat cap, a nose, a buckskin sleeve, and a gun aimed directly at his chest. Nor could he hear Susan's quick breathing and the pounding beats of her heart. He heard a hoarse voice and was too frightened and befuddled to detect the affected quality of the heavy tone. The dim light and the screen of hemlocks effectually concealed the fact that "we both" were a girl and a dog.

Bill Bassett became a man with one idea—the idea that the Green Mountain Boys were after him. Dropping his gun, he started to make a dash for home. A growling dog had hold of his leg.

"Leave your cap 'fore you go. We want that letter of Colonel West's," said the hoarse voice.

How could *anyone* on Otter Creek know he had that letter? This was too much. It was spooky. Fairly tearing the old fur cap from his head, he threw it on the ground. Anything to get out of here before he was killed or flogged!

At a whistle from Susan, Traveler loosed his hold on the trapper's leg and retrieved the hat. In that instant, Bill vanished into the woods, fully convinced that the hemlock thicket

"Drop that gun! We've both got you covered."

concealed at least two husky followers of Ethan Allen and congratulating himself that he had escaped with nothing worse than a dog bite.

For a few minutes, Susan did not dare to move from her post or lower her gun, lest the trapper, after thinking things over, should suspect that he had been fooled and return. Little did she realize how certain Bill felt that the Green Mountain Boys were lying in wait to give him the "beech seal."

Presently, seeing the rifle lying on the ground where he had dropped it, she ventured cautiously out and picked it up. 'Twouldn't do to leave the gun where he could just come back and grab it. Why, how weak her legs were! She could hardly stand up. Fairly crawling back to her shelter with the rifle, she leaned against a tree and gave in to the reaction that had set in now that the strain upon her was lessened. The arm that had kept the gun pointed so steadily at Bill was weak and numb. So were her legs. For a moment only, she relaxed. Then the rifle was at her shoulder again. Traveler had let out a fierce growl.

Anxiously she peered down the trail. No one was in sight. She turned to look at the dog. He was taking out his rage on the trapper's cap, tearing at it and shaking it furiously between growls.

"Bring it here," she called frantically, remembering the letter. Traveler, like the well-trained dog he was, promptly fetched the mangled headgear to his mistress and dropped it in her lap, then stood wagging his tail in the hope that he might have a chance to worry it again.

Thanks to the hound's assistance, the lining was partly torn out. There beneath the crown lay the letter. It was still legible though punctuated with toothmarks and torn.

Between sharp glances down the trail, Susan read:

TO THE COMMANDER OF THE GARRISON:
A report has come to my ears that that prince of rogues, Ethan Allen, may in the near future make an attack on Fort

Ticonderoga. I believe there is surely some such plan on foot, though I do not know when it will be carried out. Be ready.
From,
A LOYAL SUBJECT OF KING GEORGE

"'Loyal subject of King George,' humph!" snorted Susan indignantly. "'That prince of rogues, Ethan Allen!'" she repeated with feeling to Traveler as she gave him back the remains of the cap and stuffed the letter into her pocket. Propped against the tree, she continued to watch the trail while the hound reduced the tattered fur to mere shreds.

"What on 'arth!" Joe Barnes stopped in his tracks on the way up-creek to the Eldredge place. A strange-looking figure was coming to meet him. "Why, it's a gal, and she's got my old cap and jacket on. I vum!"

At that moment, Traveler came bounding toward him barking joyfully. "I'll be switched if it ain't Susan Eldredge," exclaimed Joe, beginning to chuckle. "What in tunket are you up to, Susan, parading around with my clothes and my gun? Ain't you growed up yet?" The chuckling ceased abruptly when he saw how white was the face framed by the fur cap.

"Oh, Joe, Joe, I'm glad you've come. Take these guns, please, 'fore I drop 'em. And do you 'spose I could git a bite to eat down to your cabin? I'm so terribly hungry."

The trapper saw that the girl was almost ready to drop with weariness. Without stopping to ask questions, he relieved her of the guns. "You come right along with me, and I'll fix you some dinner in two shakes of a lamb's tail. Got some trout I ketched this morning and half o' that pie your mother sent me. It was so licking good I come nigh eating it all up. Glad now I didn't."

"But somebody's got to stay here," she objected, looking anxiously back over her shoulder. Then, in as few words as possible, she told what had happened.

"Why the dad-blamed, sneaking little skunk!" exploded Joe. "I knowed he was in cahoots with the thieving colonel. Told your father so. We'd oughter have run him out o' here long ago."

Suddenly his spluttering rage turned to laughter. "Scared of a girl and a dog was he! Ha! Ha! Ha! Tee-hee-hee! Didn't you fool him though! Oh, Susan, you're a smart young-un. You've earned a good dinner, and you shall have it. And don't you worry your little head 'bout his coming back," he reassured her, shouldering the two guns and starting for home. "If I know Bill, he's too much of a coward to stick his head out o' the woods again. Bet he'll hide up somewheres."

Susan was silent as they walked along. It was effort enough now just to put one foot in front of the other. But the trapper was so excited he couldn't stop talking. "Jehoshaphat! What did I want to go fishing this morning for? Between us we could have took the both of 'em prisoners and tied 'em up. Now that old fox—the colonel—has got away! He's prob'ly hiding too. And I guess there's people on this creek as would take him in fer some o' those bright shillings he jingles." The girl could not help smiling at Joe's boast of what they might have done together. But it was impossible to keep her mind on his talk. Her thoughts were of fish and apple pie.

"Joe-oe, have you seen anything of Susan?" It was Mr. Eldredge's voice.

"She's alright, Mat!" shouted the trapper from the doorway. "At least she will be as soon as she's finished this pie."

"I declare, Susan," her father began indignantly as he caught sight of her sitting at the table, "if you wa'n't going on sixteen years old, I'd take you over my knee and spank you. And I dunno but I will anyway. Here your mother and I have been worrying—"

"Now, Mr. Eldredge, you hold your hosses a minute till you hear Susan's story," broke in Joe as the girl made violent efforts to speak with her mouth full of pie. "Then I guess you won't feel so much like spanking her."

When his daughter had finished her account of all the happenings crowded into that May morning, Mr. Eldredge was silent for fully a minute. "Well," he said at last, "I guess I oughter feel proud of you for what you did today, and I do. But don't you fergit this, Susan Eldredge, if you ever go chasing around these woods again, holding up men single-handed, I *will* spank you, no matter how old you are, by thunderation! I will. Another time it might not end the way it did today. Wonder you haven't been kill't 'fore this, anyhow. Now you'd better come along home and let your mother know you're safe."

The look in the father's eyes belied the severity of his reproof. When they reached home, he took her part in the family discussion of her rash adventure. Mrs. Eldredge, who at first could think only of the danger her daughter had been in, declared that "there wa'n't no sense in a girl risking her neck chasing around after Yorkers and spies. She should leave that sort of thing to the menfolks."

"There wa'n't no menfolks for her to leave this to, Mercy," he reminded her. "If she'd waited for me or Nate or Joe to git there, that sneaking trapper would have been halfway to Ticonderoga. Our own son and Jonathan Lathrop may owe their lives to Susan's risking hers this morning."

"Don't believe Bill Bassett would have ever got to Ti anyhow," objected Nathan. "The Green Mountain Boys have guards posted on all the roads to stop people from going to the fort."

"Mebbe so, mebbe not," said his father. "Bill might have sneaked over there without anybody's seeing him, much as he's traipsed around these woods. And if they had held him up, he might have fooled them. You can't tell.

"'Tanyrate, I'm going to ride Blaze to Pittsford tomorrow morning and see if I can't find somebody who'll take a message down to Bennington about this. The Green Mountain Boys ought to know what that colonel, as he calls himself, has been trying to do and how our daughter outwitted him. And you can go with me, if you want to, Susan."

The girl needed no further proof that her father was pleased with her morning's work and proud that she was his daughter.

Jonathan, who had heard Joe's version of Susan's adventures, hurried down to the Eldredges' as soon as the chores were done that evening to hear the story from the girl's lips.

"Oh, Susan! Susan! You ought to be a Green Mountain Boy too," he told her as they said goodnight on the doorstep.

"Well, anyway," she said, "I'm a Green Mountain *Girl*. That's what Colonel Allen called me. Do you remember?"

Jonathan nodded. "Guess he'll think you're the bravest girl and the smartest in all the Grants when he hears about this. That's what I think too."

His words of praise said themselves over and over in her mind, long after he had ridden Starface into the woods. They kindled a light in her eyes that even a long night's sleep did not put out. It was still shining when she woke at dawn and began to get ready for Pittsford.

Chapter XXIII

The Call at Dawn

"For the land's sakes! Who's that? Is someone trying to knock the door down?"

Mr. Eldredge jumped up, tipping over a tankard of milk and flooding the table as the thundering knock rattled the door on its leather hinges. The wooden spoonful of porridge halfway to Susan's mouth dropped with a clatter, spattering the floor. The corners of the cabin were still shadowy. In the east the sky was just growing pink. What brought anyone to their door at dawn? It must be a stranger. One of the neighbors would have walked in.

Susan's father threw back the heavy door. A haggard, white-faced man stood before him, a man who leaned against the doorpost as if exhausted and wiped drops of perspiration from his forehead, though the early-morning air was chilly. "Does Nathan Eldredge live here?" he demanded without stopping to answer Mr. Eldredge's "good morning, sir" or to accept his invitation to come in.

"He lives over there in that cabin. I'm his father. Come in and rest a spell. You look like you needed rest. Tell us, what brings you here at this hour?"

"Can't stop. Tell your son to be at Hand's Cove by nightfall. Colonel Allen's orders. Attack tonight."

Before Mr. Eldredge could even open his mouth to reply, the man was gone.

Susan pushed back her bowl of porridge and left the table. She could eat no breakfast now. Her father stood for a moment in the doorway looking out into the dewy May morning, seeing nothing, then strode across the yard to Nathan's cabin. In silence Mrs. Eldredge and the two girls cleared away the half-eaten breakfast and made the cabin tidy. Presently Mrs. Eldredge went to the cupboard and pulled out a kettle of drippings. "Girls," she said, "we'll build a fire under the big kettle and make some soap."

Susan's eyes opened wide. "Why, Mother, we've got a whole crock full of soap."

"No danger of having too much."

The girl looked into her mother's face and read in it the reason for the sudden interest in soap making. She wanted to keep so busy she would not have time to think about the work that lay ahead of Nathan that night. Susan gathered up kindling and wood and ran out into the yard to the soap kettle as though the task were one that called for desperate measures. Her father came back from the cabin beyond the spring, grabbed up his hoe, went over to the field of early corn, and began hoeing at such a furious speed that he clipped off the pale corn sprouts as well as the weeds, without noticing it.

Meanwhile, in the tiny cabin across the clearing, Nathan, in a state of wild excitement, was cleaning his rifle, filling a powder horn, rubbing bear's grease into a pair of heavy shoes, making everything ready for his first duties as a Green Mountain Boy. "Guess we'll give 'em the surprise of their lives over at Old Ti," he gloated. "My! But I'm glad I joined the Green Mountain Boys."

Deborah bent low over Nathan's homespun coat and scrubbed vigorously at a spot on the front of it, so that her husband might not see the anxious look in her white face. "Save your elbow grease, Debby," he said, laughing at her efforts. "Nobody's going to see the spots on that coat by lantern light." But she kept rubbing away at the old coat without looking up.

***

"He wouldn't even wait to have dinner. Said he didn't want to miss anything," Deborah sighed.

"So excited he don't know whether he's walking on his head or his feet," muttered Mr. Eldredge. "Hope he'll know which end of his gun to fire."

The family members were standing in a solemn little group watching Nathan as he hurried away into the woods. At the bend in the trail, he turned and waved his hand gaily. Then the trunks of the trees hid him from their sight.

"Come on, Debby. I need your help making my soap," said her mother-in-law, understanding exactly how the girl was feeling at that moment. "And Susan, you'd better fetch another bucket of water."

Susan hurried to the spring. Looking up at the "King's Mark" cut into the brown bark of the pine trees, she asked herself, "Would those straight trunks ever be masts on the king's ships now?" Probably not. The world seemed to have changed overnight. And nobody knew *what* was going to happen. Her thoughts wandered back up-creek, where they had been most of the morning. What was Jonathan doing? Had he, too, started for Hand's Cove? Suppose—suppose she never saw him again.

As she ran back along the path, a cheerful whistle sounded behind her. She set down the pail and looked into the woods, half-unconsciously supplying the words to the whistled tune as she listened:

> "Lord Lovell, he stood at his own castle gate
> A-combing his milk-white steed,
> When up came Lady Nancy Bell,

To wish her lover good speed, speed, speed,
To wish her lover good speed."

Jonathan came into the clearing walking so fast he was almost on a run, with a rifle over his shoulder.

"Hello! I'm—off—for—Hand's Cove," he panted. "Has Nate gone?"

"Yes, only a few minutes ago. You must have just missed him on the trail."

"I've got to be gitting right along. But I—I wanted to say goodbye to you before I started. Why, Susan, don't be so solemn," he reassured her as he saw how white and anxious she looked. "Taking Old Ti's going to be as easy as falling off a log. Noah Phelps, one of the men who came up from Massachusetts, was over there yesterday, pretending he'd come to git the barber to shave him. He says they don't suspect a thing."

It seemed to the girl that a weight was lifted from her shoulders. At least they wouldn't be just waiting to pour bullets down on the Green Mountain Boys. Colonel West or somebody else hadn't succeeded in giving the plan away—thanks to her perhaps, she thought proudly.

"That's better," said the boy as a faint smile curved Susan's lips. "Now don't you worry a mite about us."

"I won't worry," she promised, though she knew the promise would be broken. "Colonel Allen always does what he sets out to do."

But when Jonathan took her hand and said goodbye, her great dark eyes grew so misty she looked down to the ground that he might not see how hard it was for her to let him go. Placing his hand under her chin, the boy tilted up her face till she was forced to meet his eyes with her tearful ones. Then he did something that surprised him as much as it did Susan. He kissed her. "Now I—I've got to git along," he stammered, and before she could speak, he had started down the trail on a run.

All the rest of the day, Susan flew about, doing not only her usual duties but making jobs for herself. And all day long, her cheeks were on fire with excitement that burned within her. She fetched armfuls of wood from the pile in the yard and helped stir the brown, syrupy mass in the soap kettle. She scrubbed and scoured the kitchen floor and table until they were white, then made the flax wheel whir as she spun skein after skein of linen thread. Even the spinning wheel seemed to share her anxiety. "Going away, Miss Nancy Bell. Going away, Miss Nancy Bell," it seemed to murmur as it turned.

Mrs. Eldredge and Debby, too, scarcely sat down to get their breath. Susan noticed that her mother churned when there was not cream enough to make "dirtying up the churn" worthwhile. Out in the cornfield, Mr. Eldredge swung his hoe recklessly with a far-off look in his eyes. Even Joseph shared the excitement. He built a great fort of corn cobs in the yard and called it "Old Ti." "Green Mounting Boys are tumming! Green Mounting Boys are tumming!" he chanted jubilantly, then with a flourish of his pudgy arm sent the corn cobs flying in all directions.

"If only taking a real fort were as easy as that!" thought Susan. "With no live men and boys to be wounded and killed."

Chapter XXIV

A Long Night

All that night, a candle burned in the Eldredge cabin. Not until sunrise was it snuffed out. The only ones who went to bed were Faith and Joseph. Mrs. Eldredge, Deborah, and Susan knitted until their fingers were fairly numb. Mr. Eldredge smoked pipeful after pipeful of tobacco and paced restlessly about the cabin, until it seemed to Susan that she would scream if he did not keep still. There was little talk, for no one could think of much to say. Their thoughts were not in the candlelit room. They were out in the dark on the other side of Lake Champlain. Even the dog seemed uneasy and anxious, barking at every slight sound in the woods and getting up and following Mr. Eldredge about whenever he moved.

"Plague take you, Traveler! Lie down, and keep still," ordered Susan irritably, then patted his head to show that she did not mean to be cross. Oh! There went another stitch. That must be the third or fourth this evening. Her fingers were all thumbs. She picked up the dropped stitch, jabbed the needles into the ball of yarn, went to the door, looked out into the moonlit night, and listened, as though some news from Old Ti might be floated to her on the May breezes.

"Evening." Susan jumped. So did everyone in the cabin.

"Thought I'd find you all up. Didn't see no sense in going to bed myself," said Joe. "Seemed more sociable to smoke my pipe over here with you." The trapper's cheerful voice relieved the tension in the cabin. Susan sat down to her knitting again.

"Glad you did, Joe. We're wide awake as owls." As he spoke, Mr. Eldredge picked up a coal from the fire with the tongs and lighted the visitor's pipe.

"S'pose Sam'l Beach stopped here this morning?" asked Joe.

"A man come to the door 'bout sunup. Said Colonel Allen had sent him."

"That was Beach. He's the blacksmith down in Rutland. If we all had legs like his, the hoss traders wouldn't never do no business in the Grants. How many miles do you s'pose he traveled 'twixt noontime yesterday and noon today—all shank's mare?"

Mr. Eldredge shook his head.

"Sixty!"

"Want to know!" was all Susan's father could say.

"His tongue was fairly hanging out of his mouth when he come by my place, but he wouldn't even stop to drink the mug o' buttermilk I offered him."

Joe, the news gatherer, talked on as the night wore away, telling the little group about all the feverish activity outside their clearing, below Otter Creek and even beyond the Grants, that had been leading up to this night. Susan listened intently and found herself wondering how Joe had found time to do anything, even to keep his traps set, for the past fortnight.

He told how men had come up from Massachusetts to help plan this expedition and to take part in it and how money had been raised by Connecticut to help pay for equipment. The final plans had been made yesterday at Richard Bentley's place in Castleton, and men had been gathering at Landlord Remington's Sunday and Monday to be ready for action as soon as the hour for marching was set.

"They've sent Captain Herrick with thirty men down to the end o' the lake to take Major Skene prisoner and to git his boats."

"What's Skene done?"

"He ain't done nothing yit. But he holds that great place o' his direct from the king. So 'tain't likely he's a-going to be on the side o' the Colonists in a fight. Is it?"

Mr. Eldredge was silent for a moment. "Looks like they was expecting a real war—a real war."

"Like enough," agreed Joe, "but mebbe 'twon't last long. Mebbe King George'll sing another song, when he sees we've got our backs up."

No one spoke for a few minutes until Joe broke the silence.

"Jerusalem! I'd like to a been a mouse in the walls of Old Ti yesterday when that Massachusetts man went over and pretended he'd never had a barber shave him and that he wanted to see what it felt like. Acted kinder simple-minded. And they didn't suspect a thing—no more'n that little feller over there would." He looked toward the trundle bed where Joseph lay, sleeping peacefully, undisturbed by the event that was keeping the lights burning all night in the cabins on Otter Creek.

Some time after midnight, Susan and her mother set to work frying venison steak and making johnnycake, while Debby set the table. It seemed strange to Susan to be sitting down to a meal at that time of night, when outside everything was so dark and still. They all ate heartily, for sleeplessness and worry had made them hungry. Joe's appetite was especially good. This "owl night," as he called it, was a picnic for him. "There was no one dear to him risking his life under the cannon of Old Ti," thought Susan a little bitterly. Yet she was glad he was there chattering cheerfully. It shortened the long hours.

When the first glimmer of morning showed in the sky, Mr. Eldredge knocked out his pipe and put on his cap. "Come on,

Joe. We'll saddle Blaze and ride and tie over to Hand's Cove. There ought to be some news by the time we git there."

"Can't I ride up behind you, Father?" asked Susan pleadingly. But he shook his head. "You stay here with your mother and Debby, and we'll come back just as soon as we git the news."

Traveler, too, wanted to go to Shoreham and looked as disappointed as his mistress did when told to stay at home. But Blaze laid back her ears in disgust over being led out of the stable at such an early hour.

If the night had seemed long, the morning was even longer. Susan felt relieved when it was time to milk the cows and turn them out to pasture and feed the chickens. She and Deborah and her mother kept their hands and feet busy and talked little. Every now and then during the morning, one of them would peer out of the door toward the woods. Once Susan walked part way down the trail to see if anyone was in sight, while Traveler raced ahead of her. On the way back, he kept looking around and whining his disapproval. It was evident that he wanted to go find Mr. Eldredge and Nathan. Encircling the dog's warm body with her arms, Susan drew him close to her and stroked his long, silky ears. "Oh, Traveler!" she whispered. "I know just how you feel. I'd like to be over there too. It's terrible jest waiting, waiting, waiting and not knowing what's happened—all yesterday afternoon, all last night, and this morning." Suddenly the birds began to make frightened cries. Looking up for the cause of the commotion, the girl saw an eagle high overhead, flying into the west. Just where she wanted to go! If only she could climb on his back and ride with him across the creek and over the lake.

Sometime before noon, everyone rushed out of the cabin. They had heard the "thump, thump, thump" of a galloping horse on the trail. There was lather on the mare's brown flanks as her master rode her into the clearing, and her sides heaved in and out. But her brown eyes were bright, and her head was high as she looked at the waiting group in the yard. Perhaps she knew she brought news of a history-making event.

Mr. Eldredge's hat was in the air. "They've taken Old Ti!" he shouted. "And not a drop of blood shed! Nate didn't git there. They didn't have boats enough to take them all over. But he's gone with Captain Warner to capture the fort at Crown Point."

Chapter XXV

The Story Jonathan Told

"A Green Mountain Girl and an honorary captain of my company!" Susan repeated the title over in a whisper, then out loud, trying to convince herself that the blotted, hurriedly written words on the torn-edged scrap of paper were actually there—and in the handwriting of Colonel Allen. "Because of the bravery she has shown in a critical hour and the important service she has rendered to the Green Mountain Boys."

"It's a captain's commission. He wrote it himself this morning and told me to be sure that it got to you," explained Jonathan, seeing how dazed Susan looked. "You're a captain in the Green Mountain Boys. You're my captain," he added with a smile.

The smile grew, as he saw how the girl's eyes danced. "Susan Eldredge, Captain of the Green Mountain Boys." She repeated the words now for the sheer pleasure of hearing them. "I shall keep it always," she said, looking with awe at the signature—"Ethan Allen, Commander of the Green Mountain Boys."

Again Susan and Jonathan were sitting on the rock under the pine trees. Again he had come whistling along the trail through the woods, and she had run to meet him, anxious to be the first to hear his story.

As for Jonathan, he had hurried straight from the fort to the Eldredge pitch, partly because he bore an important letter for Susan from his colonel but even more because he wanted to tell his story of the capture of Old Ti to her before anyone else had heard it. He wanted to watch—with no one to distract his attention—the shining of her dark eyes and the flaming of her cheeks as she grew excited. All the way from Shoreham, he had been telling her the story in his imagination and seeing her eager face as she listened.

"If it hadn't been for you, I probably wouldn't have got across the lake at all, 'cause they didn't have half boats enough," he said when the letter had been tucked away for safekeeping deep in the pocket of Susan's dress.

"If it hadn't been for me!" The girl's eyes widened with excitement.

"Yes, Colonel Allen picked me out of the crowd when he was loading the boats. He remembered seeing me at your house that day. ''Pon my word,' he says, 'it's Susan Eldredge's friend Jonathan. Jump in, lad. You look like you'd be handy with a pair of oars.'"

Now the words began fairly to tumble over each other as Jonathan told how Fort Ticonderoga was captured "easy as falling off a log." The pine trees stirred restlessly and murmured an accompaniment to his words. Perhaps in all the centuries they had kept watch above Otter Creek, they had never heard a more exciting tale.

"Guess I won't forgit rowing across the lake, long's I live—dipping the oars as quiet as we could and talking in whispers and all of us jumpy as grasshoppers. Another thing I'll always remember is that wait we had in the woods this side o' the lake, watching and watching for boats to come.

"I tell you, I was worried for fear everything was going to fall through, jest for want of boats. And the whole plan hung on gitting there mighty quick 'fore anybody found out what we were up to.

"When it got along past midnight, and we jest had one boat and an old scow, Colonel Allen started to walk up and down and swear under his breath. Then we knew there was really something to worry about. Finally he decided to start out with as many men as he could take.

"Jest as we was ready to go, that man from Connecticut bobs up again and says he's going to lead the men."

"What man from Connecticut?"

"Oh, I forgot to tell you about him. He was a Colonel Benedict Arnold, all prinked up in a grand uniform with shiny buttons, bringing a servant along with him. He'd showed up down at Castledon. Said he'd been given the command of the expedition by the Massachusetts Committee of Safety. Well, the Green Mountain Boys down there said they'd joined to take the fort under Ethan Allen, and if Colonel Arnold wanted to take the fort, he'd have to git his own men and they'd go home. That settled his hash. At least they thought it did. But the hash didn't stay settled long.

"Here he was taking precious minutes to argue, when it was gitting later and later every second.

"Well, the thing had to be decided and decided quick. So Ethan said they'd march into the fort together.

"While we rowed acrosst the lake, the sky was beginning to turn gray above the trees, and a rooster was crowing somewhere. I was all gooseflesh by that time. It was 'bout three o'clock. 'Twould be daylight in no time at all, and there weren't more'n a third o' the men on t'other side.

"Then Ethan, he lined us all up and counted us. There were only eighty-three. He said our 'valor had been famed abroad'—'famed abroad,' that was what he said—and that this morning we must either take the fort in a few minutes or fail in what we had promised to do and 'quit our pretensions to valor.' 'It is a desperate attempt,' says he. 'Only the bravest men would dare to do it. I urge no one to come against his will. But those of you who are willing to, poise your firelocks.' Quick as a flash, every man of us raised his gun.

"And we set out, stepping soft like Indians. Jerushah! Weren't we excited when we went through the wicket gate in the wall and walked right up to that dark old fort."

In imagination, Susan crept along the parade ground in front of the silent fortress with Jonathan in the gray half-light of dawn. In imagination, she saw the sentry raise his musket and aim it right at the tall colonel. "I don't believe one of us breathed. We expected to see Ethan drop dead. But the musket missed fire. Then we made a rush on the guards 'fore they could do any more firing." The girl seemed to hear the great whoops that rose from the lips of the men outside the fort and went echoing down the lake. With them, she rushed up the stairs to the captain's quarters and saw a lieutenant come to the door wide-eyed and confused by so sudden and rough an awakening from sleep. She was there listening eagerly when Ethan Allen roared out his demand for the surrender of the fort and the startled man asked, "By what authority do you make such a demand?" There thundered in her ears Ethan Allen's answer, "In the name of the Great Jehovah and the Continental Congress." Oh, she could just hear him say it!

All the rest of her life, it would seem to Susan as though she had been at the fort that night and helped to capture Old Ti, so vivid was the story Jonathan told while the ancient pine trees whispered above their heads and a brown thrasher sang as though he could not contain himself for delight.

When the story was ended, the boy and the girl on the rock were silent for a few moments. Jonathan cleared his throat nervously and began poking the pine needles with the butt of his rifle. "Er-er—Susan. Do you know what I was thinking about when we went through that gate to the fort?"

... crept along the parade ground ... in the gray half-light of dawn.

Susan of the Green Mountains

She shook her head.

"I was thinking of how you looked when you said goodbye—how you were crying."

"I wasn't crying," she denied indignantly. "I was jest—jest excited and—all upset—about everything."

There was another silence—one of those uneasy silences. "Mebbe it was silly of me," Jonathan began again, "but I sorter hoped you were thinking of me, too."

"I was. I thought about you all night," she admitted.

"Well—what I mean is—I mean—" floundered Jonathan, "I was thinking that I wanted to come back; I didn't want to git killed, because of you."

He broke off and poked the needle-strewn ground furiously for a minute, sending indignant beetles scurrying for cover, then tried to say what was in his mind in another way. "While we were waiting over there on the lake in the dark, I built a cabin 'twixt our place and yours. That is, I imagined I was building it, laying the logs jest so and chinking it so's it would be tight and cozy in cold weather and making chairs and tables and beds for it. And—and—I could picture you jest as plain sitting by the fire in that cabin. You see, Susan, I was building it for you."

He raised his eyes from the ground and saw that the girl was looking up into the swaying branches overhead and smiling dreamily. "I can see it too," she said, "and I can see you bringing in a backlog for the fire."

The smile that began in Jonathan's eyes in a moment had set his whole face aglow with happiness. "If you can see it too, someday when we're a little older and this rumpus with the king is settled, I'll start building it."

The girl and the boy under the pine trees could not look ahead and see how their courage and their steadfastness of purpose would be sorely tried before that cabin would be built. Neither did they dream of the changes that would take place in their wilderness with the passing of time. If only they might have pictured themselves in the years ahead, living in a frame house and driving a carriage over real roads! If only they might have foreseen that the quarreled-over Hampshire Grants would become the state of Vermont, where settlers were undisturbed by Yorker rivals! They could know neither the sorrows nor the joys in store for them. Yet, because they had come safely through bitter hardships and great perils in the past, their faces turned hopefully toward the uncertain future.

THE END